Letting Ana Go

Letting Ana Go

Anonymous

Simon Pulse

New York London Toronto Sydney New Delhi

ᗯᗯ

SIMON PULSE

An imprint of Simon & Schuster Children's Publishing Division

1230 Avenue of the Americas, New York, NY 10020

First Simon Pulse paperback edition June 2013

Copyright © 2013 by Simon & Schuster, Inc.

All rights reserved, including the right of reproduction in whole or in part in any form.

SIMON PULSE and colophon are registered trademarks of Simon & Schuster, Inc.

Also available in a Simon Pulse hardcover edition.

For information about special discounts for bulk purchases,

please contact Simon & Schuster Special Sales at 1-866-506-1949 or

business@simonandschuster.com.

The Simon & Schuster Speakers Bureau can bring authors to your live event. For more information or to book an event contact the Simon & Schuster Speakers Bureau at 1-866-248-3049 or visit our website at www.simonspeakers.com.

Designed by Lissi Erwin

The text of this book was set in Adobe Caslon Pro.

Manufactured in the United States of America

10 9 8 7 6 5

Library of Congress Control Number 2012956565

ISBN 978-1-4424-7213-6 (pbk)

ISBN 978-1-4424-7223-5 (hc)

ISBN 978-1-4424-7214-3 (eBook)

Letting Ana Go

Friday, May 18

Weight: 133

Breakfast: Bagel (toasted), light cream cheese, orange juice (fresh squeezed! Thanks, Mom!).

A.M. snack: (Who has time for this?) Jill gave me a Life Saver in English. (Does that even count?) It was green.

Lunch: Turkey wrap with Swiss cheese, SunChips, Fresca, ½ bag of gummy fruit snacks.

P.M. snack: Other ½ of the gummy fruit snacks.

Dinner: Lasagna (1 square), Caesar salad with croutons. Dad made brownies. Ate two.

Now I'm supposed to "write a few sentences about how I feel." I feel this food diary is strange, and sort of funny. When Coach Perkins handed them out brouhaha ensued. ("Brouhaha" was a word on my final vocab quiz of sophomore year today. As was the word "ensued.")

Coach Perkins passed out pamphlets at practice. Not really pamphlets but I like all those *p*'s. Journals, actually.

Coach: It's a "food diary."

Vanessa: What is this *for*?

Geoff: Why don't I get one?

Coach: Only the ladies.

Coach said girls on other cross-country teams have been

using our sport to hide their eating disorders. They run until they collapse from not eating enough, not drinking enough, not knowing enough. Hello? Dingbat? Running four to eight miles per day? You're going to need some calories. (At least two brownies after dinner.)

Naturally, the adults are only now catching on. They thought that's just what runners look like. Parents: sometimes clueless.

As a result of not eating, these girls get sick, and we girls get to write everything down.

Our food.

Our feelings.

I still feel it's funny, somehow . . . or maybe absurd. (Also on the vocab quiz.)

Not Vanessa: This is unfair! What about the guys?

Or Geoff: Yeah! This is cool! I wanna do it too!

Ugh. Lovebirds. Too cute = puke.

(COACH PERKINS: If you're actually reading this, that was a figurative "puke" not a *literal* "puke.")

Coach says she'll be checking the diary every practice, and then over the summer when we meet up to check in once a month before school starts. Coach Perkins is pretty.

Ponytail, push-up bra, probably pushing forty. Not one to be trifled with. Tough as nails.

Jill was painting her nails in my room after practice during our weekly Friday-night hang out. I told her about the food diary, and how I found it preposterous.

Jill: Please. I've been keeping one for six weeks.

Me (laughing): WHY?

Jill: So I can lose ten pounds.

Me: You'll disappear.

Jill: Shut up.

Me: Seriously. You already look like a Q-tip on toe shoes.

Jill: The Nutcracker Nemesis must be vanquished.

Me: You're losing ten pounds for *Misty Jenkins*?

Jill: I'm losing ten pounds for *me*. I will be Clara this Christmas or you have seen my last pirouette.

She blew on her nails and looked at me with the same wide-eyed stare she has presented each Friday night past when making pronouncements of epic proportions over popcorn. These are not to be pooh-poohed, and I made the mistake of laughing.

She pounced with a pillow.

A brouhaha ensued.

Saturday, May 19
Weight: 132

Breakfast: Dad's omelets—eggs, cheddar cheese, tomatoes, bacon.

Vanessa and Geoff came over this morning and we ran before breakfast. Dad cooked us all omelets afterward. Mom was still in bed because she gets off so late at the hospital. I don't know how she stays awake enough to give people medicine in the middle of the night, but she says you get used to it. I turn into a pumpkin at about 11 p.m. every night.

Dad was doing his cooking tricks because Geoff and Vanessa were watching. He can toss eggs over his shoulder and catch them and break them into the bowl with one hand. He was spinning the whisk around his fingers and juggling tomatoes. He was a short-order cook before he started selling cars and he loves an audience. I've seen all his moves before, but Geoff and Vanessa were cracking up. It made me feel good— proud of my dad. He never went to college or anything, but we have a really nice house and great cars and everything because he's so smart and worked his way up until he was able to buy his own dealership.

I texted Jill and she walked over while we were eating. Dad tried to get her to have an omelet but she would only eat a bite of mine, then immediately pulled out her phone. Vanessa and I had just been saying we didn't know how we were going to remember every single thing we ate every single day without carrying these food diaries around with us all the time, and Jill smiled and waved her phone at us.

She was using this app called CalorTrack, which helps you keep track of what you eat. Everyone who uses the app can go online and enter the nutritional information and serving size of the foods they are eating. In the app, you can search for the food you have just eaten or are about to eat and it records the calories. You can set goals to lose weight or gain weight, and it charts your progress online. You can even print out a report of what your calories are over a week, or a month. This was a revelation. Vanessa and I immediately downloaded this app. Naturally, Geoff did too. Dad watched us all being absorbed into our phones and started doing the funky chicken dance in the kitchen using oven mitts as wings to see if he could distract us. We all started laughing at how ridiculous he looked. Jill and I had tears running down our faces.

I like Dad so much when he's in a good mood. I can't even be mad at him for behaving in a way that is completely and utterly mortifying because he's so funny.

Mom wandered into the kitchen, bleary-eyed, in her sleep pants and T-shirt. She saw Dad and started laughing with us. She kissed my head, and Jill and Vanessa said good morning, but when Dad saw her it was like somebody threw ice water all over him. He stopped dancing and started doing dishes. I don't think anyone else noticed.

Except Mom.

I don't know why Dad won't let her be part of the fun. He handed her a plate with an omelet without smiling, and turned back to the sink. Mom sat and talked to us while she cleaned her plate, but I couldn't take another bite. I just wanted Dad to come sit down with us.

Mom: These are so good! Dale, come sit down and have one with us.

Dad: (grunt from sink)

Geoff: His cooking is almost as good as his dancing.

Vanessa: Do the funky chicken again.

Mom: I always miss the good stuff!

Dad (under his breath): Not much of it . . .

No one heard Dad but me because I was sitting closest to the sink, and because Geoff was trying to demonstrate the funky chicken dance. Mom laughed at Geoff's attempt, then asked me if I was going to finish my omelet. Dad turned around and shot daggers at her. He opened his mouth to say something, but then glanced at Geoff and Vanessa and Jill, and turned around again.

Me: It's all yours, Mom. I'm stuffed.

Dad didn't think I saw him roll his eyes, but I did. How can he go from somebody I love to somebody I hate in the span of four minutes?

A.M. snack: Nothing. (Still full from breakfast. Dad's omelets are huge.)

Lunch: Tuna fish sandwich with tomato, carrot sticks, BBQ potato chips.

P.M. snack: YouGoYum yogurt—chocolate swirl, small, with bananas, pecans, chocolate chips, and hot fudge.

After her rehearsal at City Youth Ballet, Jill texted me and asked me if I wanted to get yogurt. She drove by my place and picked me up, her hair in the signature bun of ballerinas everywhere. YouGoYum is one of those "pump it yourself" places that seems to be sweeping the nation. There's even one in my grandma's town, a wee town with a single stoplight where the Starbucks recently closed. I chose a small cup and took pride in my perfect loops of classic vanilla-and-chocolate swirl. Making a picture-perfect soft-serve cup topped by a tiny twist like the ones in TV commercials requires both patience and precision. When I'm successful it pleases me beyond words.

I placed my yogurt on the scale at the register and turned around to see what Jill was having. Her fingers held only her phone, upon which she was typing out a text message.

Me: Where's your yogurt?

Jill (pointing at mine): Right there.

Me: You aren't getting anything?

Jill: Just a bite of yours, thanks.

Me: But . . . you texted and asked if I wanted to come get yogurt with you.

Jill (wide-eyed pronouncement face): No, I asked if *you* wanted to get yogurt.

Me: That bun is restricting blood flow to your brain.

Dinner: Buster's Burgers—junior double cheeseburger with ketchup, tomato, lettuce, mayo, crinkle-cut french fries, Diet Coke, half a chocolate shake. (Split it with Dad.)

I get the family-tradition aspect, but I'm not sure why Dad still insists on Buster's Burgers every Saturday night. Lately, every time we go, he gets all hot and bothered if Mom orders a burger that isn't "protein-style" (no bun), or we'll be standing in line and he'll start saying things like, "Wow! That new Garden Chicken Salad looks great! You want to try that, Linda?" He says it in this voice like he's never *seen* a Garden Chicken Salad before, as if he can't *imagine* such a thing, full of wonder and awe and a tempered excitement as if at any moment, he may simply *explode* with the rapturous joy of grilled chicken and tomatoes on a bed of mixed greens. It's the voice I suspect scientists used when they first saw satellite photos of the rings around Saturn.

It is the most annoying thing in the world.

News flash: if you are so concerned that Mom eat a salad with lo-cal dressing on the side, maybe Buster's Burgers isn't the place to come for dinner every Saturday night. Just a thought. I'm almost sixteen years old. Our family unit will undoubtedly survive if we take a weekend off.

Mom sat there across the booth from me picking at her wilted greens, watching Dad munch his BBQ Bacon Double Trouble and drink his thick, dark beer while he plugged quarters into the tiny jukebox they have mounted on the wall over every table. When he got up to order another one at the counter, Mom snuck a couple of his fries and scrunched up her eyes at him like a little kid who was going to do something she shouldn't just for spite. That made me laugh, and I was still giggling when Dad walked back to the table and wanted to know what I thought was so funny.

Mom: I was just telling her about our first date here and how you wore those snakeskin boots and black jeans you thought were so rock 'n' roll.

Dad: They *were* rock 'n' roll back then.

Mom (to me): They were so tight he could've sat down on a penny and told you if it was heads or tails.

Dad: And I could still fit into those jeans.

What he meant was *you* couldn't fit into what you were wearing back then. Of course, he didn't actually have to say those words. He just looked at her the same way he did at breakfast this morning when she ate the rest of my omelet. Nobody talked on the car ride home, but I knew the silence was the calm before the storm. When we got home I kissed them both good night in the kitchen, and before I got to my room, the terse whispers had exploded into an all-out battle. Name-calling, dish clattering, counter banging, door slamming, the usual. Our usual. I caught words here and there:

Late shift

Hospital

Lard ass

Disaster

So mean

How could you

Not with a ten-foot pole

Cleaning lady

Pigsty

Secretary

Finally, I put on my headphones and pulled the covers over my head to drown out the rest. I've heard it all before.

Sunday, May 20
Weight: 133

Vanessa texted me and came over to run before Mom and Dad woke up. I snuck past Dad, who was sleeping on the couch, and met her in the driveway. We ran by Geoff's house and he joined us for a five-miler. When we got back to my place, Dad was headed out to the dealership. Sundays are big sales days. He grinned as he saw us coming up the drive, but I couldn't smile back. I hate it when he and Mom fight. I was sweaty and gross, but he insisted on a hug, and told me he'd left us a surprise on the counter for breakfast. . . .

Breakfast: Two doughnuts: one round glazed, one chocolate long john.

Mom woke up while Geoff was polishing off the last of the doughnuts and Vanessa and I were stretching in the living room. We were watching an episode of this reality show we love where drag queens redesign each other's bedrooms. It always devolves into somebody throwing a wig at the camera. Mom paused and looked at the doughnuts but didn't have one. In fact, she didn't eat anything, just sat on the couch with us staring at the TV until the show ended and Geoff left to walk Vanessa home. I was starving again and made an ...

A.M. snack: Protein smoothie with strawberries and bananas.

There was extra left in the blender, so I offered a glass to Mom. She shook her head. I asked her if she was going to eat anything and she just looked sad and told me she needed to save her calories for dinner. I asked her if she was writing down what she was eating. She sighed and didn't say anything. Mom has this big, epic, end-of-the-world sigh. It's almost as annoying as Dad being a jerk about what she eats. If you want to change something, change it. Don't just sit around sighing all day like a balloon losing air. I feel sorry for Mom, but not as sorry as she feels for herself.

Lunch: Deli turkey and cheese slices, rolled together like little burritos. Wheat crackers, baby carrots dipped in ranch dressing.

I was studying for our biology final tomorrow. Stopped to enter all the stuff I was eating into the app on my phone. When I punched in two tablespoons of ranch dressing I was astounded. The little dollop of dressing had more calories than all of the carrots and turkey I ate *combined*. How is that possible?

When I took my plate back down to the kitchen, Mom was standing in front of the refrigerator holding the package of cheese slices. I saw a bag of potato chips on the counter.

Me: Want me to make you some turkey roll-ups?

Mom: No! I told you I want to save my calories for dinner.

Me: Just because you don't put the food on a plate doesn't mean the calories don't count.

Mom: *SIGH*.

P.M. snack: None.

I got lost in a biology blackout. I didn't even think about eating until I heard the garage door opening. Dad was home and brought barbecue takeout with him. The smell made my mouth water and I ran downstairs. He was grinning ear to ear as he laid out ribs and pulled-pork sandwiches, coleslaw, and baked beans on the island in the kitchen.

Dad told us the new salesperson he lured away from another dealership was already the best producer this month. He said she's already sold more cars in two weeks than his top seller sold all of last month. Mom did a double take when he said the word "she."

Dad: What?

Mom: *SIGH.*

Dad: Are you going to eat with us?

Mom: Yes. I've been very good all day today.

Dad: I can make you a salad if you want to keep it up.

Me: *Dad.* Lay off. She hardly ate anything all day.

Dad: I'm just trying to *help*.

Mom: *SIGH.*

Dinner: Six baby-back ribs, baked beans, coleslaw, half pulled-pork sandwich.

We ate in the living room. Dad wanted to watch this zombie show on cable, which was fine until the last five minutes, when six of the undead jumped out of the woods and chased the hero's wife across a grassy country field. When she got hung up in a barbed-wire fence and ran out of ammo she had to kill the last one by jamming the gun in its skull. Thankfully, I was finished eating by then. Mom was still holding a baby-back rib, but she yelped, then put it down and pushed her plate away.

Zombie shows and barbecue: not a good recipe for dinner, though perhaps a good way to diet.

After dinner I went back up to my room and tried to study

for biology some more, but everything ran together in front of my eyes, then my phone buzzed with a text message:

Jill: Biology brain bleed. Help me.

Me: Ur text = last thing I saw. Blind. Pls send future texts in Braille.

She called me laughing and said her head was going to fall off. I told her I was officially a member of the phylum Exhaustica. There was a lot of noise in the background and she was shouting into the phone. I asked if there was a tornado at her house. She explained her brother, Jack (yes, her parents named their children Jack and Jill—as Mom would say: *SIGH*), and his friend Rob were studying vocabulary for their Spanish final. Jill thinks Rob is the hottest guy on the soccer team.

Me: Sounds like some pretty aerobic studying.

Jill (yelling): Rob read some article online about retaining things more quickly if you're doing something physical while you memorize information. They are kicking a Nerf soccer ball back and forth down the upstairs hallway.

Me: And you're watching Rob run past your door as a studying technique?

Jill: He's so cute.

Me: It sounds like a crop duster.

Jill: Rob's calves are so sexy.

Me: Fourscore and seven years ago, our fathers brought forth on this continent a new nation, conceived in liberty.

Jill: Totally. Have you noticed Rob has this little divot in his chin that—

Me: I'm hanging up now. Enjoy the view.

I'm pretty sure Jill talked to me for at least five minutes after I hung up before she realized I wasn't there anymore. I love her, but I'm no match for Rob's legs. Mom walked by on her way to her bedroom and told me there was clean laundry for me in the dryer. I went down to get it, and Dad grinned and waved me over to the couch. He was eating . . .

Dessert: Five bites out of Dad's Ben & Jerry's pint.

Ironically, Dad's favorite flavor is Chubby Hubby. Of course, he's not chubby at all. He's in great shape. He goes to the gym three or four times per week and lifts weights and runs on the treadmill. He used to run half marathons, and still talks about training again. He was watching some talk show with a politician and some comedians on it. They were in front of a studio audience and kept zinging each other, then sipping something out of mugs with the show logo on it. Zing! (Sip.) Zing! (Sip.) Zing! (Sip.)

We watched the show and passed the pint back and forth.

After five bites I held up my hand. Dad took one more big bite with a smile, and then paused the DVR. He put the lid back on the ice cream, then got up and put the pint in the freezer. He asked if I was ready for finals. I pulled a throw pillow over my face and collapsed on the couch.

Dad: What?

Me (muffled by pillow): I hate that question.

Dad (laughing): Why?

Me (throwing pillow at him): Because how the heck would I know if I'm ready? You never know if you're ready for a test until you are actually *taking* the test in question.

Then we both cracked up and Dad said he was sorry, that he would never ask if I was ready for a test again. I like him so much sometimes. I wish he were as nice to Mom as he is to me.

Monday, May 21

Weight: 134

Breakfast: Raisin bran with soy milk, orange juice.

A.M. snack: Nothing.

Lunch: 2 tacos—ground beef, lettuce, tomatoes, cheese, Spanish rice. Fresca, split a Twix bar with Jill.

P.M. snack: Trail mix from the vending machine: almonds, dried cranberries, raisins, white chocolate chips.

Dinner: Leftover lasagna (one square), spinach salad with tomatoes, avocados, and balsamic vinaigrette.
Dessert: 100 Calorie Snack Pack of mini-Oreos.

The best parts of today ranked in order of excellence:

1. Biology. Is. Over. For. Ever. (And I think I did okay on the final.)
2. Taco bar for lunch.
3. At practice, Vanessa showed Coach Perkins the CalorTrack app and we gave her our printouts from the last few days. Coach said we could continue using the app, and could bring our printouts to her during our summer practices.

Jill came over to study for our English final tonight. Dad worked late at the dealership and Mom leaves for the hospital around 4 p.m. She usually works four twelve-hour shifts every week. I was making leftover lasagna and a salad when Jill arrived in her post-rehearsal warm-ups. I offered her lasagna but she'd only eat salad. And by salad, I mean the raw spinach leaves with tomatoes—no avocado or dressing. We reviewed the English study guide for a long time, then we reviewed how hot Rob's legs are for an even longer time. If there were a final on Rob, Jill would ace it.

Thursday, May 31
Weight: 132
Breakfast:
A.M. snack:
Lunch:
P.M. snack:
Dinner:
Dessert:

I've been keeping track of my calories on CalorTrack for the past week since Coach gave us the go-ahead, but I just saw this food diary while I was cleaning out my bag. I realized there's no place in the app to write about our feelings. I guess Coach Perkins forgot about that part of the assignment. Not that it matters so much to her about how we feel, although that makes her sound like a terrible person, and that's not what I'm saying. I just meant the point of her having us keep track of our food intake is so we stay at a healthy weight for running. I'm sure she doesn't miss having to wade through all of this babbling.

I guess I sort of miss writing it all down.

There's something about seeing my words on these pages from the past week that gives me a feeling inside I'm not sure how to describe. It's like when Mom tells me I have to clean out my dresser drawers because they are such a jumbled mess she doesn't know which one is for socks and which one is for underwear or T-shirts. I hate the feeling of dread, which starts with me basically dragging myself into my room by force and dumping out the drawers on my bed. It feels like an impossible task—like I'll never get everything folded neatly and put back into the dresser.

But then, little by little, it just happens—one T-shirt at a time—until finally, I slide the last drawer into place, and then I feel a big wave of relief in my chest. For the next few days at least, I try to keep the drawers as neat as possible. I become extra-diligent at folding things up when I put them on and don't wear them, and I make sure to put everything back in the right drawer, tucked away just so. Having a clean dresser affects my whole room, too. It makes me not want to leave my clothes on the floor at night. I always try to put them in the hamper, or hang them back up. I guess it sounds ridiculous, but I love that feeling I get in the morning when I open my eyes and everything is put away.

Of course, eventually, I get in a hurry, or I'm running late, or I can't decide what to wear on the way out the door and change twelve times, and then I come home to an avalanche of stuff to deal with. If I don't do it right away, the dresser gets messy again in a hurry—I just start shoving things wherever they'll fit. But while it's clean it seems I have all this space and freedom in my room, like the bedroom itself is bigger and has more space and air.

It's the same way with this food diary. Today was the last day of school, and I dragged home all the crap from my locker. I was unpacking my book bag in my room, and when I saw this diary, the first feeling I had was how glad I was that I didn't have to write in it anymore. Still, I flipped it open and read over some of what I'd written, and all of a sudden, I felt this urge to write again—like somehow it would be sad if I just stopped. It's only been a little more than a week and I'd already forgotten about telling Jill that her bun was too tight when we went to get yogurt, and it made me smile to remember that. I wonder what else I've forgotten because I didn't write it down?

As I looked back on all the pages I'd written so far, it was like seeing clean dresser drawers in my brain, and my heart. It's like I've taken this tangled mess of thoughts and feelings and things that happened and stuff people said and folded each one carefully into a little entry about what happened that day.

So I dug out a pen. The minute I was holding the pen in my hand, it felt impossible to write anything down. Then I saw the first blank for my weight, so I weighed myself and wrote that down. I've already typed all of my food into the app so far today. I decided to skip all that and just write what is going on today.

Today, my sophomore year is officially over. Next year, I'll be a junior. Vanessa got all weepy when we were cleaning out our lockers because she and Geoff won't see each other every single second of every single day anymore, although that's not really the case. We'll be running together practically every day, and usually we hang out in the afternoons, too. Geoff will probably get a summer job working construction for his dad a few days a week. I promised Vanessa that we would go and take him lunch if she wanted to, which made her smile and wipe her eyes.

She said it wasn't just Geoff she'd miss, it was *this*, and then she waved her arm around the hallway.

I don't know how to explain it, but I knew what she meant. We'll be back in school in twelve weeks—same buildings, same hallways, same people—but we'll never be sophomores again, and we'll never take biology together again, and we'll never be exactly the same as we were right in that moment. This afternoon when she said it, I understood what Vanessa meant, but now that I'm thinking about it, folding it up in these sentences and sliding it into the drawer with all my other thoughts and memories, it makes a knot swell up in my throat and my eyes sting a little bit. Who knows how this summer will change us?

I guess this is one of the reasons I like Vanessa so much. She remembers how special these little moments are while we're still having them.

I'm glad that I decided to write this down. Now that I'm

finished, it feels like I have all of this brain space left over to use for thinking about other things. I don't have to worry about forgetting this either. It's all right here, tucked neatly away for the next time I need it.

Friday, June 1

It felt so nice to sleep in this morning and not have to go to school. Coach Perkins ran us hard yesterday because it was our last practice before summer, and I was sore when I walked downstairs. I poured myself a bowl of Lucky Charms and plopped down in the corner of the sectional and flipped on the TV. Last night was Mom's fourth shift, so she'll be off for the next three nights, but I tried to be superquiet because she's always exhausted from working four nights in a row.

I was catching up on this show Jill and I always watch where this comedian cracks jokes about videos from the Internet. He's really tall, and skinny, and he's not drop-dead gorgeous or anything, but he has this handsome smile and he's so funny that he's one of those guys who gets cuter and cuter the longer you look at him. Sometimes he shows videos where somebody breaks an arm, and I have to fast-forward through them. You can always tell it's coming, just from the setup. Usually it's somebody on a bike getting ready to ride down a set of stairs, or some idiot pulling a bozo in a shopping cart behind a pickup truck. The thing Jill and I are always amazed by is that most of the time, you can tell that the person who is in the video doing something completely deranged is also the *person who uploaded this video*. Which begs the question, why would you want the *entire world* to see you do something so stupid? Isn't it enough that you came two inches from death and wound up in the hospital with a cast on your leg? Must you advertise this fact? When I do something that's embarrassing, I just feel like dying. I want to curl into a tiny ball and crawl under my bed.

Anyway, Mom stumbled into the kitchen and said good morning. I smiled and she came over and kissed me on the top of the head, then walked back across the great room and stood in front of the open refrigerator for what seemed like forever. Then I heard her *SIGH*. After that, the pantry opened, then closed. Then the cabinets next to the refrigerator opened, then closed. Then the pantry again. Then another *SIGH*.

And finally, I couldn't stand it one moment longer. I turned off the TV and marched into the kitchen with my empty bowl, rinsed it out in the sink, dried my hands, turned to my mother (who was peering into the refrigerator again), and said:

Mom! This is ridiculous. Just eat something for breakfast.

Mom: But I'm so fat. I just need to save my calories for dinner tonight.

Me: Stop. Whining.

Mom (shocked): Wha—?

Me: You are not fat. You need to lose twenty pounds. You are a *nurse*. This is not rocket science.

Mom: But I've been trying to diet and . . .

Me: Mom, dieting doesn't work. You *know* this. This is about changing the way you eat. Calories in versus calories out.

Mom: But I don't eat that much!

Me: No, you do eat that much, you just don't know what you're eating because you don't sit down and make a meal. You graze all day long and pretend that you're saving your calories for dinner, but really, you're eating all these little bites of crap all day, and then eating way too much at night because you're hungry from not eating the right stuff during the day.

She started crying at this point, and I gave her a hug, but I am just tired of this. Dad's always giving her a hard time about it, true, but if you want to fix something, you just have to start somewhere.

Me: How much do you weigh?

Mom: I . . . I don't know. I'm afraid to look.

Me: Jeez!

I grabbed her hand and dragged her up the stairs to her bathroom. I pulled the scale out from under the sink and pointed to it. I told her I wasn't leaving until she weighed herself. I quoted Coach Perkins. She said, just like performance in a sport, weight is one of those things you have to measure. Coach Perkins always tells us if you don't know where you're starting from, you don't know where you're going, and only the things that get measured get changed.

So she stepped on the scale. Honestly, it wasn't as bad as I thought, but she needs to lose about twenty-five pounds. At that moment, Jill rang the doorbell, and we went back downstairs. She saw that Mom had been crying and asked if everything was all right. I told her it was, and then Vanessa and Geoff showed up. We are all going to the pool at the club Jill's parents belong to today to lay out and get our tans going for the first day of summer. Right there in the kitchen every single one of us whipped out our phones and showed Mom CalorTrack. I downloaded the app on Mom's phone while Jill set up her account on the laptop and Vanessa showed her how she could type in the first few letters of the things she ate every day and they'd pop up on the list. Before we left for the pool, we helped her set a goal, and Geoff confiscated most of Mom's stash of Snack Packs and lo-cal treats and low-fat everything as snacks for the pool.

Vanessa pulled some cottage cheese out of the fridge and measured a three-quarter-cup serving. Jill cut up a cantaloupe that was sitting on the counter. Geoff put water in the electric kettle and brewed some tea. Then I went and got my swim stuff while they kept her company and talked about what she could eat for a morning snack, and lunch, and an afternoon snack.

Finally, everybody piled into Geoff's car, only I ran back inside to get my sunglasses, but couldn't find them. As I was digging through the junk drawer under the key hooks at the kitchen island, Mom grabbed me around the waist and squeezed me extra tight. She whispered the words "thank you" into my ear really softly.

I kissed her cheek, told her to be sure to eat lunch and take a walk, then ran for the car. As Geoff pulled out of the driveway and Vanessa cranked up the music, Jill reached over and handed me my sunglasses. I put them on and she smiled and said, Welcome to Your Summer. We're So Pleased You Could Join Us.

Then Geoff let out a whoop and sped down the street.

Monday, June 4

As I picked up the pen to write this I realized my cheeks were aching because I've been smiling all day.

This morning I ran the mile and a half to Vanessa's place. Geoff was already there, stretching in the driveway, and we did a middle distance at a pretty fast pace. When we ran by my place I went in and showered, while they ran back to Vanessa's. Mom was sitting at her laptop entering her breakfast meal—half a grapefruit, egg whites, and one piece of whole-grain toast. She looked up and smiled at me, and for the first time in as long as I could remember, she seemed excited about something.

I kissed her on the cheek and she pointed at the screen to where she'd just entered her weight from that morning. She's already down one pound since she started keeping track last week! I gave her a high five, and she giggled.

After I got cleaned up, Geoff came by and we drove over to meet Jill at her parents' club again. They've got such an awesome pool with a couple of springboards, and the snack bar is to die for. Jill got all As last semester, so as long as she gets permission her parents let her sign for all of our food on their account. It's not that we eat a lot or anything, but it's a great deal. It's one of the reasons we studied so much last year. Jack and Rob were with her, and Geoff challenged them to a cannonball duel to see who could splash the most water out of the pool onto Jill, Vanessa, and me. Naturally, the results were hilarious and disastrous with Geoff, Jack, and Rob ultimately being called into the head lifeguard's office. I, personally, had been unaware of the lifeguard hierarchy at the Fielding Club Aquatics Center until today, but suffice it to say watching the Cannonball Splash-O-Rama (as Geoff called it) being referred up the chain of command in a series of stern warnings and whistle blowing over approximately two hours was among the funniest things

I have ever witnessed. While Jack was being threatened with a suspension of his membership privileges at the pool by a red-nosed sophomore from the local junior college named Rusty, Rob and Geoff were firmly tutored in the Guest Behavioral Guidelines by Becky, the "assistant head lifeguard." A curly-haired woman who coached the club's master swim team, she made it clear that if the guys continued to give "her staff" any more trouble, they would be put on the Fielding Club Aquatics Center watch list for the next month and not be allowed into the facility as a guest.

All of the cannonballing and lecturing had made the guys hungry, and after our run, I was starving myself, so we went to the snack bar. When we arrived, Rob gave an order to Jack that was roughly as long as the Bill of Rights, then he and Jill went to nab us a table on the sundeck that overlooks the lap pool. Jack called after her to see what she wanted to eat, but she just shook her head and waived her bottle of water at him.

Jack: She never eats at the pool, does she?

Me: Did you just meet her today?

Rob: I'll get her to eat a nacho if it kills me.

Jack: It may.

Rob: Dancers and runners, world's fittest women everywhere I turn.

Geoff: We are some lucky bastards, aren't we?

Me: Like the three of you can talk. Your abs belie your 8 percent body fat.

Rob laughed, and walked as quickly as he could without drawing a whistle from a lifeguard. He joined Jill, who was pulling up enough chairs for all of us around a single table in the corner.

As we stood in line under the snack bar awning, Geoff draped his arm around Vanessa's shoulders and she leaned into him. His chin sat perfectly on top of her dark, wet ringlets. They were doing that thing they do where they somehow tune out the entire world by touching each other, which left me standing there next to Jack, suddenly shivering in the shade. I crossed my arms over the top of my suit. I've had breasts for a couple years now, but I don't need to be shivering and flashing my high beams at my friend's older brother in front of God and the world.

Jack's hair was still wet, and he tossed his bangs out of his eyes with a little flip of his chin and smiled at me.

Jack: You cold?

Me: A little.

Jack: I'd put my arm around you like Geoff here is doing for Vanessa, but that might be weird.

Me (laughing): Yeah. Might be.

Jack: Although, I hate to see you shiver like that.

Me (taking two giant steps out from under snack bar awning): Maybe I'll just stand over here in the sun and wait for you to get the food.

Jack (loudly): Yeah, but now I feel lonely.

Me: We regret to inform you that your loneliness has been trumped by our lack of body heat. We sincerely apologize for any inconvenience and look forward to seeing you in the sunshine again very soon.

Jack's laugh was infectious and I couldn't resist joining him. It was strange. In all the years Jill and I have been best friends, I don't remember being around Jack without her being right there with us. Standing there laughing, six feet apart, him in the shade, me in the sun, it was like I was meeting somebody new. Right before he stepped to the counter to order enough nachos and Red Vines to sink a submarine, he flipped his wet bangs off his forehead again, and for the first time ever I noticed his eyes.

As blue as the bottom of the pool.

Wednesday, June 6

Dad took me to dinner tonight. Mom is working shift three of four.

When I was little he used to do this Dad and Daughter Date Night where we'd go eat pizza and see a movie. I can't remember when we stopped doing it. I think around the time I went to middle school. I started running track that year, and Dad got the opportunity to open the dealership. It's one of those things you never mean to stop, but you don't notice when it does. Then one day you look up and it's over almost before you realized it was happening.

We went to this Korean barbecue place downtown where you cook your own meat on the grill in the middle of your table. It was delicious and we ate until we were stuffed. I thought about how much Mom would have liked this place. I wondered why he never brought us here. He'd obviously been here before. He knew the hostess by name, the waitress asked how things were going at the dealership, and the chef came out to make sure everything was okay.

Dad read my mind: I come here for work lunches a lot.

Me: It's a long way from the dealership for lunch, isn't it?

Dad: Yeah, but it's such great food. Sometimes it's worth the trip.

I remember a lot of things about our Dad and Daughter Date Nights when I was little. I remember the place we used to go for pizza with the stage full of singing puppets at the end of the dining room. I remember putting a dollar bill in the machine and the *kerchink* of tokens tumbling into the silver tray. I remember the feeling of Dad's arms around me as he helped me toss the

Skee-Ball into the 100-point hole. I remember squealing with excitement as the endless tape of tickets came spouting out as the sirens rang and the lights flashed. I remember the candy and tiny monkey doll for which I exchanged the tickets. I remember the doll was fuzzy and brown. I remember how she sucked her hard plastic thumb in a perfectly round, hard plastic mouth.

I don't ever remember Dad lying to me on one of our Dad and Daughter Date Nights when I was little.

This was a first.

Dad scribbled a tip and a signature across the credit card slip, then pocketed his card and headed for the door as if he were being chased. Just like that I looked up and saw our dinner was over—almost before I realized what was happening.

Saturday, June 9

It began as a cookout.

It turned into a freak-out.

It ended in a walkout.

First there was Dad firing up the grill, and me turning up the music, and Mom whipping up the fixings. She was whistling as she seasoned that ground beef and smiling to herself as she rolled it into balls and smashed them into patties.

I knew she was feeling good about herself. I can't really tell the four pounds are gone, except when I look in her eyes. For the first time in a long time, she's got that twinkle back. She doesn't look tired. She looks as if she's remembered some sort of good news she'd almost forgotten about.

The smell of the burgers was making my stomach growl as I carried the place mats and utensils out back to the patio table by the grill. Vanessa and I ran this morning even though Geoff slept in. I knew I'd have to eat two burgers to hit my calorie goal for the day, and that was fine with me.

Mom raised her can of Fresca once we all sat down: To my beautiful daughter, whose beautiful friends helped me start to feel beautiful again.

I laughed: Oh, please, Mom. You're beautiful all the time.

Mom: I was telling your dad I've lost four pounds already by keeping track of everything in that app you showed me.

Me: I'm very proud of you, Mom.

I looked at Dad. I looked at Mom, who was looking at Dad. Dad was biting into his burger as if nothing was happening at the table, as if nothing important was being said, as if it didn't matter that Mom had lost four pounds.

As if he didn't care.

I saw the hurt in Mom's eyes as she reached for the tray of burgers and wrapped hers in lettuce instead of a bun. She gave a halfhearted laugh and told me this was "protein-style," without the carbs.

Dad asked me how far we ran this morning. He asked me what we'd been doing since school got out. He laughed when I told him about the Cannonball Splash-O-Rama and the "assistant head lifeguard."

I reached for a second burger and another slice of cheese: These are delicious, Mom.

Mom winked in Dad's direction: Well, your father sure can cook on a grill.

Me: You should have seen him at the Korean barbecue place. He's practically a pro.

The minute the words left my lips, Dad looked up and stared into my eyes. It was a hard stare, one that said he wished I hadn't said what I'd just said.

Mom and I both said, "What?" at the same time. Me to him. Her to me. She looked at Dad and said she'd always wanted to go there, but he'd always said he was afraid they served mystery meat. I turned to her and told her about our Dad and Daughter Date Night on Wednesday. How Dad is like a celebrity at this place downtown. Something in Dad's stare told me to shut up. Something in Mom's eyes told me to keep going.

I could hear the words coming out of my mouth, but it was like someone else was saying them—like I couldn't have stopped them if I wanted to:

He knew everybody's name.

The chef came to our table.

It was delicious.

The waitress asked about the dealership.

He goes there all the time for lunch with clients.

There was a strange silence when I finished. It lasted for what felt like forever. Mom reached for another burger. This time, she took two slices of cheese and a bun.

She gave me an awkward smile: I've been so good this week.

I felt Dad's long, cold stare leave my face as he shook his head: Not *that* good.

I'd never heard my mother curse before today. Never once. Nor had I ever seen her throw anything besides a towel, into the hamper. The burgers must've still been pretty hot because Dad yowled like an alley cat when they hit him in the face, and the ceramic platter bounced off his chest and broke across his knee. As the pieces clattered to the concrete patio and shattered into a thousand bits I had the sudden thought that we'd never be able to put this back together if we tried, and as Dad raced into the kitchen for a towel to stanch the blood pouring from his knee and Mom yelled words I'd never heard her say before in a voice I could not recognize, I slowly climbed the stairs to my room, closed the door, and put on my headphones.

I fell asleep listening to a singer I love who plays the piano in a minor key over wailing guitars. Her voice is full and lush and I dreamed of falling endlessly backward into a rich velvet darkness.

When I woke up Dad was gone.

Mom was sitting on the couch, staring at the television screen with the sound muted, eating a pint of Dad's Chubby Hubby. I sat down next to her, and she tried not to look at me, but I could see her eyes were almost swollen shut from crying.

I put my arm around her shoulders: Is it over?

She nodded: Yes.

I'd always wondered what it would feel like if my parents split up. Sitting there, holding my mother as she buried her face in my shoulder and cried until my T-shirt was soaked, I didn't feel anything at first. Somehow, it made a strange sort of sense. It seemed this wasn't about me. This was about them. So shouldn't they be the ones with the feelings? Wasn't it right for my mom to be the one crying?

Then I felt something wet and cold against the leg of my jeans. The ice cream Mom was holding had melted and was oozing out of the container, a thick, cold pool across my thigh. Something about it made me gag. We were a mess. This was a mess. I was covered in tears and mascara and stickiness. I pushed my mother away from me, grabbed the carton and the spoon from her hand. As I ran to the kitchen, a chill went up my spine as her tears trickled down my neck and over my clavicle. I looked back at her as I wiped the ice cream from my jeans and washed the stickiness from my fingers and arms. In a flash, I felt something:

Disgust.

And guilt for feeling disgusted.

And certainty that we'd never be able to put this back together—even if we tried.

Sunday, June 10

I can't stop crying. I can't eat anything. I don't know why. It's not like they were such a barrel of laughs when they were together. Jill showed up and rang the doorbell because I turned off my phone. She sat in my room on the bed and didn't say a word for three hours. Just handed me Kleenex while we watched reruns of that Internet video-clip show with the comedian. It's one of the reasons Jill is my best friend. She knows when to be quiet.

I even watched the broken bone videos. Didn't bother me at all.

Monday, June 11

Vanessa and Geoff came over to pick me up for our first summer cross-country practice. They barely noticed I wasn't really speaking until we got to the parking lot at school. Vanessa just kept talking about this movie they went to see last night and how awful it was. How the lead actress is supposed to be a teenager in love with a zombie slayer but couldn't even move her mouth. Geoff parked and turned around to do his impression of her happy face, her surprised face, and her sad face, which were all the same face. I started laughing, and then burst into tears like one of those girls I hate. I am not a public weeper. Vanessa is a public weeper.

I told them about my parents. Vanessa was shocked about what had happened, shocked that I hadn't called her, simply *shocked*. (She can really be a drama queen.) I assured her I was fine.

Vanessa: You don't look fine.

Me: You wouldn't have answered your phone anyway.

Vanessa: What's that supposed to mean?

Me: Nothing. You were in a movie. Can we please just drop it?

Vanessa: Um, your parents just split up. I don't think that's something we can drop.

I told her I was far more worried about these stupid printouts. I haven't been able to eat anything in two days. Vanessa and Geoff assured me Coach would understand, although I didn't see how. Either I had eaten enough or I hadn't. Why would my parents or my feelings have anything to do with it?

But they did.

Coach Perkins isn't exactly the touchy-feely type. She has a very finely tuned BS meter, and the second she saw me, she asked me what was wrong. Her exact words were: You look awful.

Something about the way she said it made me laugh. I *did* look awful. I thrust my CalorTrack printouts at her. I told her I hadn't been eating. She pulled me aside and asked me if I was upset over a boy.

Me: Kind of. My dad left.

Coach: I'm sorry.

Me (starting to cry): I'm not.

I've run cross-country for Coach Perkins since the summer before freshman year. For the first time in two seasons, she wrapped her arms around me and hugged me until I pulled it together.

She said: You don't have to run today.

I said: Yes, I do.

Tuesday, June 12

I told Geoff and Vanessa I needed a day off from running this morning, but really I needed a day off from them. I didn't sleep very well, and when I woke up in the gray light at six thirty this morning, I clamped my eyes closed again as if I could shut out the day, but it was too late. The feeling in my stomach, the one that won't let me eat much, seems to kick-start my brain into hyperdrive:

Who was Dad taking to that Korean barbecue place?

Why wouldn't he take Mom?

Why would he lie about it?

Why didn't Mom try harder to lose weight sooner?

Why didn't Dad try to be kinder and help her?

Why did he have to leave?

Does he still love me?

I can never let myself go like Mom did.

But she works so hard.

Still, that's no excuse.

My mind seemed to be on a runaway raft in the middle of a river, bouncing down level-five rapids, until eventually, it tossed me out of bed. I didn't know what else to do before 7 a.m., so I pulled on my running shoes and put in my earbuds.

I ran in the opposite direction of Vanessa's house just in case. I ran toward the mountain, staring up at the top of the peak, turning down my thoughts by turning up the music, and letting the cadence of my feet on the pavement focus my breath in a steady rhythm: in-two-three-four, out-two-three-four, in-two-three-four, out-two-three-four. Breathing in for four strides then out for four strides gave me something to focus on besides the thoughts crashing through my head, and then the sun must've broken over the horizon behind me, because it drenched the mountain with a splash of crimson across the top that bled into the indigo at its base. There was something so big about the mountain canvas, and so bold in the colors, that all I could do was drink them in with my eyes like a thirsty little girl with a cold glass of grape Kool-Aid.

My eyes began to water and tears mingled with the sweat running down my temples onto my cheeks. These tears were different from the others I'd cried since Sunday. They weren't directed at my dad or my mom. These tears were squeezed out of me by the colors of the sun's brush on the sky, and clouds, and rocky peaks. These tears streamed out of me in answer to the magnitude of what they saw. I ran for farther than I might have otherwise, if only to keep the mountain in my vision, and by the time I turned around to run back home, I felt very small against the massive summit. What a tiny speck of dust I am compared to the rest of this universe. I could no more control the colors of the sunrise than I could my mother's weight, or my father's roving eyes.

I realized the only person I can control is me, and as I turned the corner down my street and headed for my driveway I realized one more thing:

I was hungry.

Jill was waiting for me on the porch. It was almost 8 a.m.

and I couldn't believe she was even awake, much less dressed and waiting on the stairs.

She smiled and waved: There you are. I've been texting since dawn.

I opened the front door and she followed me to the kitchen, where I gulped down a glass of water, then rounded the island into the den to stretch on the carpet. I asked her if everything was okay.

Jill: Better than okay. Don't be alarmed.

Me: You understand my concern? It is a summer day before 10 a.m. and you seem to be showered, clothed, and in your right mind.

Jill: I bring important news.

Me: By all means, share.

Mom wandered into the kitchen right at that moment looking out of sorts. She was rumpled and dazed. Ever since I left her sitting on the couch Sunday, she jumps when she sees me as if she's startled, as if she's forgotten I'm here. She turned suddenly when she realized Jill was with me, then stopped and slowly turned back around, continuing into the kitchen to open the refrigerator door. She took out a carton of cottage cheese and bravely tried to smile at Jill. It was almost convincing.

Jill smiled and said good morning, and Mom asked what

the important news was. Jill told Mom it was a good thing she was here, because it concerned her, too.

Jill: Mom and Dad are letting Jack and me each bring a friend on our annual boat trip at Lake Powell this year.

I should note here that Jill squealed this information, which was startling. Jill is not particularly known for any sort of girlish excitement. She is typically droll and measured. Also, it was early for squealing.

I grimaced: So, who are you going to take?

Jill: *You!*

This was also a squeal, but Jill was bouncing up and down on her knees, which made me feel extremely fond of her, so I couldn't frown. In fact, as I pulled my left calf toward my chest in a stretch, I felt my mouth spread into a smile across my face, and turned my head to look at my mother.

Mom had opened the cottage cheese over the sink and appeared to be staring into it for the answer to an unasked question. So I asked it.

Me: Mom, can I go?

Mom: Huh—?

Me: Can I go with Jill to Lake Powell when they go on vacation next week?

Mom (blinking): Oh. Oh, sure. Yes.

Jill: (SQUEAL)

Me: Mom, are you sure you'll be okay?

Mom: Yes. Yes, of course. I'm fine. It'll do you good to get out of the house.

I smiled and stood up. Jill threw both arms around my neck and jumped up and down, causing me to move with her, and as she squealed I couldn't help it: I laughed, and for the first time since Saturday, I felt like maybe the world wasn't coming apart at the seams.

Mom smiled at us jumping up and down in the living room. This was the first true smile I'd seen from her in four days. She glanced back down at the cottage cheese, then said, screw it, and dumped the container into the sink.

Who wants breakfast? she asked.

Mom grabbed her keys and a baseball cap she sometimes wears when she plants impatiens in the flower bed by the pool, then she drove us to IHOP and ordered chocolate chip pancakes for each of us.

To my complete and utter amazement Jill cleaned her plate.

Friday, June 15
Weight: 128

We're leaving tomorrow. I'm excited, but nervous—about going, about staying, about Mom and Dad, about being basically naked for a week on a boat with Jack. Jill says she always wears a bikini with shorts on the boat, and just slips off her shorts when she gets in the water. I've seen pictures from this trip. Usually they go with her cousins from Arizona, but this year her cousins are going to Mexico or someplace. When I asked Mom if I could have some money to go shopping for a couple new pairs of shorts and a bathing suit, she handed me her debit card and told me the PIN without looking up from the papers she was sorting through from the lawyer. I asked her if there was some sort of ballpark figure she'd like me to stay within for budgeting purposes. She looked up at me and blinked, then back down at the papers and said something about how my dad could afford it.

I walked down the driveway to get into the car with Jill. Jill was far more pragmatic about the situation and wore her "buy them both" face a number of times at a number of different cash wraps two days in a row. In the end, I have three new pairs of shorts, a new one-piece, and three new bikinis, two with trunk shorts, one with little ties on the sides. Jill insisted I get it. She said I've never looked better than I do right now. I was in the bathroom trying everything on when I got home tonight and weighed myself. I've been forcing myself to drink protein smoothies for the past week because my stomach is still too upset to eat anything. When I handed Coach Perkins my printouts today she patted my shoulder and told me I was making a good effort, but I know I'm nowhere near close enough to the number of calories she wants us to be eating. I told her I'd be on the boat all this week and she said she thought that was a good idea.

Coach: Take a break from running.

Me: I'll sort of have to.

Coach: Didn't want you making laps around the lake or anything.

Me: I hadn't thought about that.

Coach: Don't. And eat lots of chips and pizza and laugh a lot.

Jill said she's paring down her calories starting tomorrow because she won't be rehearsing. She did say we could do her "aerobics routine" on the boat. Whatever that is. She said she'd show me, but the idea of dancing around in place drives me crazy. That's the thing about running I love: I get to *go somewhere*.

Maybe that's why I'm nervous. I'll be stuck on a boat in the middle of a lake. With Jill's mom, who is nice, but let's face it, maybe a little . . . ice queen? She's like one of those blond politician's wives: hair always up, makeup always perfect, nothing out of place, eagle eyes—doesn't miss a thing.

I feel sort of guilty for leaving Mom, but she hasn't been

able to complete many sentences since the lawyer dropped off the divorce papers on Tuesday. She's plowed through two different sets two different times, initialing, crossing out, underlining, writing notes in the margins. She told me we're keeping the house. At least Dad isn't going to make us move.

Thinking about that makes me want to leave right this second. I want to be out of here and away from all this. I have to go to sleep now. I'm not sure how I'll do that. Jill and her family will be here to pick me up at 6 a.m.

Saturday, June 16

It's a nine-hour drive to Lake Powell. Jill's dad rented an SUV so large I'm not sure how we're going to make it without stopping for gas every twenty-nine miles. Rob and Jack were firmly ensconced in the very back seat when they rolled into our driveway this morning at 5:55 a.m. They were both wearing noise-canceling headphones, and their faces were obscured by flat-billed baseball caps with NBA logos and gold stickers proclaiming the size still affixed to the bills. They looked like extras from a music video.

Jill was comatose in one of the captain's chairs. She gave a grunt and tried to smile when I opened the van door, but it was halfhearted at best. I'm pretty sure she was asleep again by the time her dad pulled out of the driveway.

Mom worked last night to get some overtime, so I tiptoed into her room and kissed her on the cheek at five forty-five. She stirred and muttered something about waiting twenty minutes after I ate to go in swimming. I giggled and whispered: I love you. I'll text you when I get there.

Susan and James, Jill's parents, are as awake as I am. Her dad smiled like a news anchor when he tossed my bag behind the seats where Rob and Jack are sleeping. He said Jill was really jazzed that I could come. Jazzed. I don't think Jill has ever been "jazzed" about anything, or if she had indeed felt "jazzed" she would most certainly never have used that word. Still, I couldn't help smiling when her dad said it. When we were all settled in, he leaned over and kissed Susan on the lips—maybe a little longer than was entirely necessary—then glanced into the rearview mirror and said, "Head 'em up, move 'em out," as if he were a cowboy.

Jill groaned and readjusted her angle in the seat. The boys behind us remained silent, slack-jawed, and completely indistinguishable. Susan rolled her eyes and smirked, then turned back to me and sighed: Can you believe this guy?

I thought about my own dad. I thought about how clever and funny and charming he could be, and how more often than not, he was none of those things—like he was purposefully keeping it from us when my mom was in the room. It made my stomach turn with a familiar wincing pang of longing, a longing for something I'm not sure my parents ever had. Did my dad ever kiss my mom for a little too long? I tried to remember.

Of course, my mom never looked like Susan. She had perfect makeup at 6 a.m. Not too much makeup like a Real Housewife, just precision eyeliner and mascara, and possibly some powder? Her skin was luminescent in the glow of the dome and dashboard lights. Her platinum-blond hair had been flatironed and twisted up. She looked a lot like the wife of that old guy who ran for president a few years back—lean and pretty, but somehow pointy around the edges. My mom's edges are all soft and full, and usually straining at the fabric somehow. Susan's entire essence appeared tailored to fit even (somehow) in a predawn appearance. She offered me a bottled water and quietly chirped about how I had my own climate control for the vents above me in the armrest to my right, and how we'd stop for a bathroom break and coffee and snacks around ten; told me to just let her know if I needed anything, and in the meantime to try to relax and get some sleep because we had a long drive ahead of us. It was not entirely unlike the speech a flight attendant gives before the plane takes off, and I almost expected her to explain how to fit the metal buckle of my seat belt into the latch, and what to do if we experienced an unintended loss of cabin pressure.

I tried not to compare her to my mom any more, but it was difficult. My mother's instructions upon leaving for any sort of journey forth into the world typically consisted of the words "Hurry up, we're late," but Susan impresses me as someone who has never been late, or hurried, or wrinkled, or flustered, or held her breath to zip her jeans, or arrived with a shiny forehead ever in her life.

It's no wonder James kisses her like he does.

The sun has turned the sky above the highway the color of a forest fire. Soon it will peek over the horizon. I'm finally feeling sleepy and the thrum of the tires against the pavement and the perfectly cooled air spilling out of the vents is soothing somehow, and I think I might be able to sleep for a little while. I feel my whole body beginning to relax. I guess I didn't realize how tense I've been at home. There's a warm ease about sinking into this leather seat. Somehow I know I can close my eyes here and be safe even though we're speeding down the road at eighty miles per hour. As long as I'm here with James at the wheel and Susan riding shotgun, I don't have to worry. Everything is very clearly under control.

Later . . .

We're here! Finally. Lake Powell is the most amazing thing I have ever seen. I'll write more about that later. Anyway, we rolled in around 4:30 p.m. and went to the place where our houseboat rental was waiting. James signed some paperwork, and then we all loaded our stuff on board. Jill's parents have the master stateroom on the lower level. Jill and I put our bags in one stateroom on the main deck, and Jack and Rob took the other, but Jill says the guys usually sleep on these big cushions on the upper deck under the stars. I just wanted to write that we got here. I'm not sure why, but I feel this anticipation in my chest, an energy I'm not sure what to do with. I'm trying to figure out if I'm scared or excited. Maybe both?

The motor just roared to life, and the boys started whooping. Jack poked his head in the door. He has changed into a striped tank top and board shorts, and says I should put down my pen right this second and come to the upper deck or I'd miss my first sunset on the lake.

Later . . .

Jack was right about not missing the sunset. I followed him up the stairs to the top deck. We stood at the rail next to Jill and Rob. The engine was loud and the vibrations made my feet hum as the wind whipped through my hair. Jill smiled at me and I pushed my sunglasses up on my nose.

Slowly, Jill's dad maneuvered the boat out of the cove and

around the side of a sheer rock cliff that glowed the molten color of hot lava. As we made the turn, I saw the sun, blazing low on the water's razor edge. Fiery beams shot toward us across the flat surface of the lake, smearing orange and red across a bright blue summer sky crowned with clouds the color of royalty.

It took my breath away. I felt the radiant heat flash across my face and bore into my skin. My eyes watered at the brightness and the beauty and Jill must've heard me gasp, because I felt her hand over mine on the rail. Rob stood on the other side of Jill, and I felt him brush my shoulder as he placed his arm around Jill's shoulders. We watched in silence, the wind on our faces as the sun began to sink below the cliff line, almost as if someone had flipped a switch. As the four of us stood there transfixed I felt Jack's bare arm brush lightly against mine. I caught my breath again but didn't dare look at him. I felt my arm tense as he leaned against the rail, but he didn't move away, and I relaxed into him ever so slightly.

As the sun dropped out of sight completely, we made our way into the middle of the lake and heard people on two other boats in opposite directions far across the water clapping and cheering nature's fireworks. Rob and Jill joined in and we heard James whistling at the wheel one level below. Jack didn't move his hands from the rail to clap, and I didn't either. My heart was beating fast as I stared out across the purple sky, bruised from the blistering glory of the sunset. The buzz of the engine that I'd felt in my feet spread across my entire body, emanating now, it seemed, from the muscles of Jack's arm, taut and warm against my own.

No one was looking when he leaned closer and whispered two words into my ear: "So beautiful."

I nodded, and started to tell him it was the prettiest sunset I'd ever seen, but when I turned to face him, he wasn't looking at the sky.

I felt my cheeks flush, and I was suddenly glad I'd put on my sunglasses. Jack's eyes were kind and full. I tried to will my tongue to work, but I couldn't move or speak, until finally, Susan peeked her head over the top step of the upper deck and called to all of us, "Who's hungry?"

Sunday, June 17

Last night at dinner, we all helped Susan unload the coolers and boxes of food we picked up at the grocery store near the marina. She'd brought a few things from home and has the stocking and distribution of the boat's tiny kitchen down to a science. She unloaded and directed and pointed and explained like a well-oiled machine until the food was put away and the coolers whisked out of sight. Rob and Jack were shown where their stash of junk food was stored, along with a strict warning about breaking into supplies for family meals.

To that end, a menu has been posted on the refrigerator. It's laminated. (Just saying. Susan is like one of those women who has her own cooking show.) It maps out food for the week and I saw we'd be docking at a couple of restaurants along the way for dinner. The menu also stipulates which meals Jill's parents will be cooking and which ones will be "do it yourself" affairs. This mainly happens at lunch. Jill explained that those are times when we'll all just make sandwiches out of deli turkey or salads from the fresh organic romaine Susan brought in a cooler from home. Jill also noted that Jack typically consumes his own body weight in Twizzlers and Lucky Charms.

(How do guys eat *so much* and not gain a *single pound*?)

Anyway, after we got the kitchen unpacked, James fired up the grill and Rob and Jack were put in charge of flipping burgers and turning hot dogs. It was your basic cookout except Susan and James had flutes of champagne while grilling and white wine with dinner. There were bottles of Pellegrino and Mexican Coke ("no corn syrup," Susan said with a sniff) for everyone, and disposable silverware that was actually silver. Even the plates and napkins were thicker and more absorbent than the crinkly paper and Styrofoam my mom usually buys. We ate sitting on the top deck. There's a table that folds up next to the bench seats around the railing. I'm sitting on one of them now writing this, while Jill tans on one of the big cushions that stow away in cabinets but are big enough to sleep on. Jack and Rob slept up here last night. Jill was secretly thrilled when Rob tried to get her to sneak up after her parents went to bed:

Rob: C'mon. It'll be so romantic under the stars.

Jill: Until my mother catches me and tosses you overboard.

Rob: I'm a good swimmer. I'll risk it.

Jill had laughed and went back to . . . well, sipping Pellegrino. I swear that's all she consumed last night. It might be all she had yesterday, period. I realized she took a hot dog with no bun and cut it up into tiny pieces, and pushed it around in big pools of ketchup and mustard. She fed a couple pieces to Rob, who remarked that her plate looked like a battle reenactment, but I'm pretty sure she didn't actually have anything to eat. At all.

And come to think of it, when we stopped for coffee and lunch and snacks for the guys on the way out here, Jill always ordered a drink, but I can't remember her actually eating anything. At Starbucks she got a Venti iced coffee with two Splendas and poured a dollop of nonfat milk into it.

The thing is, she's still on her phone checking CalorTrack at least once an hour, and I'm curious. What is she keeping track of? I know she's really working hard in ballet and last night her mom mentioned seeing Misty Jenkins and her boyfriend Todd when she was coming out of the grocery store back home. Jill rolled her eyes and moaned.

Jack: What?

Jill: I will not dance behind her in *The Nutcracker* one more time.

Rob: My sister says she has a mustache. Last week Misty came into the salon where I worked and had her lip and cheeks and arms waxed.

Me: Her arms?

Jack: That's one hirsute ballerina.

Jill: Hirsute?

Rob (laughing): You think *your* vocab quizzes were hard this year? Just wait until Frau Schroeder gets ahold of you this fall.

Jack: You'll beat Misty out for Clara this fall, Sis. I know it.

Jill: If I don't, I'm not dancing.

Susan: Well, you've never been in better shape, honey.

Me: No kidding. You haven't eaten a carb since Christmas.

Susan: You know, they say that carbs are killing us.

Rob (stuffing an entire brownie into his mouth): Bring it on.

James: You deserve to be Clara because you're a fantastic dancer. Just because that girl is a stick figure doesn't mean she can sell it.

Jill: Thanks, Daddy.

Susan (raising her chardonnay): To Jill in the role of Clara.

Rob: And to mustachioed Misty. She'll make a great Sugar Plum *Hairy*.

Everybody laughed, and drank, and then Jill excused herself, headed in the direction of the bathroom down the stairs from the top deck. As she went, I saw the glow of her phone on her face.

Jack just climbed up the ladder on the side of the boat and told me I should jump in. Maybe he's right. I've been sitting here writing while he and Rob jump off the top of the boat into the water, then climb back up. Jill is lying here with her darkest sunglasses on pretending not to pay any attention to Rob, but I know she's watching him. He and Jack are both already completely tan from the pool and as they climb up the ladder their board shorts cling to their legs, pulling the waistbands lower and lower and . . .

Well . . .

Frankly . . .

It's distracting.

Later . . .

Jill brought a *scale* onto the *boat*.

I repeat: a *scale* on *vacation*.

We just went downstairs to get more sunscreen and water. I went into the bathroom and when I came out, Jill was standing on the scale in our room.

Me: What are you doing.

Jill (looks down at scale, back at me, blinks): Is this a trick question?

Me: You brought a scale with you on vacation?

Jill: My body doesn't know it's on vacation. It doesn't magically stop turning calories into pounds because we're on a boat for a week.

Susan poked her head in the door at this precise moment. She went up to the roof deck holding a bottle of water and a paperback book with a very shiny cover, all legs and sunscreen and visor and sunglasses. She smiled at us, then asked Jill how things were coming along.

Jill: Doing well. Holding steady.

Susan: I'm very proud of you, Jilly Bean.

Jill: Every time you call me that I die a little bit inside.

Susan (laughing): You'll always be my little bean, darling. I'm glad to see you fighting for what you want. That Misty doesn't stand a chance.

Susan turned to leave, then stopped and looked back at me: And *you* are a *good friend*. Jill tells me you've been keeping track of your calories, too. It's always easier when you've got support. It certainly has paid off. You've never looked better.

I opened my mouth to explain that I was keeping track of my calories in the opposite direction—making sure I got *more* calories, not fewer—but something about the look on Susan's face stopped me. The beaming smile, the admiration, it felt warm on my skin like the sun up on the top deck.

I smiled back at her and shrugged: What are friends for?

Susan winked at me and said she wasn't the only who had noticed.

Jill: *Mom!* Please!

Susan: What? Of *course* Jack would notice. I mean, look at the figure on this one. All this calorie counting and running is working out very well.

Susan put down her water bottle and book and draped an arm across my shoulders. She said she knew things must've been hard around home lately. I didn't really want to think about what was going on with my parents, much less talk about it, but Susan has this way of looking at you like you're the only person in the world who matters. Something about her smile makes you want to tell her everything. She should be a talk show host. Or a detective.

Me: I guess heartbreak is good for the abs.

Susan (laughing): That it is, sweetheart, that it *is*. But you hang in there, and keep doing what you're doing. All that baby fat has disappeared, and if you keep at it, you'll be turning every head in the hallway come fall. Jack will have his work cut out for him.

Jill must've seen me blush because she stepped off the scale, handed Susan her book and water bottle, and began pushing her out of our room.

Susan (laughing): Okay! Okay! I'm going.

Once she was gone, Jill turned to me and apologized.

Jill: Sorry about that.

Me: It's not a problem. She was just being sweet.

Jill: I haven't lost a single pound in the last two days.

Me: Is that a problem?

Jill: Yes. I've plateaued. You, on the other hand, look fantastic. When was the last time you weighed yourself?

Me: Not since our chocolate chip IHOP debacle.

Jill stepped off the scale and pointed to it. I sighed and stepped onto the square glass platform. The digital display flickered, then froze at 126.7. Jill screeched.

Jill: I can't believe it. You've been practically gorging yourself to keep running.

Me: Not so much lately. I haven't been hitting my calorie goals. I'm supposed to eat at least 2,500 to 2,800 calories on the days I run, and 2,000 to 2,500 on the days I don't.

Jill: Dear God. That's like an entire extra meal. Hope you're hungry.

Me: Well, I don't want to balloon out while I'm on the boat. I mean, I'm not running at all this week.

Jill said she was limiting her calories this week to 1,700 per day, and pointed out that it wasn't too far off from my 2,000-calorie "rest day" goal. She grinned and asked me if I thought I could do it with her.

I didn't know exactly what to say. Not being around my mom and dad and the unending sadness at our house for only two days had brought back my appetite. I hadn't been able to eat much for a week, and now that I could actually eat again, the idea of controlling it just because I could felt exhilarating. Besides, it was only three hundred calories less than I'd have been eating anyway, and I'd only be doing it to help Jill.

I nodded: Sure. Let's do it.

Jill: Excellent. You know, this is exactly what successful people do when they come up against hardships in their lives.

Me: Wait . . . what do they do?

Jill: They take *control.*

Me: Of three hundred calories?

Jill: It's a start.

Monday, June 18
Weight: 127

Jill is hard-core about the scale and the calorie tracking. I guess I knew she was doing it, but being on this boat with her and sharing a room is pretty intense. She insists we weigh ourselves before we go to bed, and again after we get up.

Sorry, scratch that. When we get up, *after* going to the bathroom. She made me redo it this morning because I hadn't pooped yet.

Jill: That's just extra weight that's going to come out of you anyway.

Me: I'd really like to not talk about my bathroom habits with you.

Jill: Go do your business and come back.

Me (fingers in my ears): LA-LA-LA-LA-LA.

In the end she was correct. I weighed less afterward.

You wouldn't think three hundred calories would make that much difference, but it *does*. It was the difference between eating dessert last night and just having some tea while Jill and I watched Jack and Rob scarf down s'mores they made over the grill.

Tonight we're docking and going ashore for dinner at this restaurant in the marina. I had two hard-boiled eggs and a cup of strawberry yogurt for breakfast this morning. According to CalorTrack that's 412 calories. For lunch the guys made deli sandwiches and Jill and I had turkey-and-cheese roll-ups. Each turkey slice had twenty-five calories and each cheese slice had eighty, so I used half a cheese slice with each piece of turkey and had six roll-ups for a total of 390 calories. That means if I stick to our plan of 1,700 calories per day, I've only got 898 calories left, which should be plenty for dinner tonight.

The problem is this: I'm hungry *now*, and it's only *two in the afternoon*. How am I going to hold out for another *five hours* until we get to the restaurant at seven tonight?

Jill and I are drinking so much water we've already run through a whole case of water bottles and we're going to stop to get more at the grocery store in the marina tonight. After lunch we were all floating on these big rafts tethered to the boat and Jill kept going inside to use the bathroom. Jack was making fun of her for not just peeing in the lake.

Jack: You have a bladder the size of a small walnut.

Jill: I will not pee in this lake.

Rob: Why not? The fish do.

Jack: So does Rob.

Rob (pushing Jack off the raft into the water): We won't tell anyone, I promise.

Jill: As a thinking vertebrate possessing the power of speech, limbs with which to climb a ladder, and a noted absence of gills, I will not be relieving myself in the water.

Jack climbed back onto the raft next to me as Rob followed Jill up the ladder to get a Coke and switch playlists on the iPhone playing through the speakers on the deck.

Jack: You having fun?

I smiled and nodded: It's beautiful here.

Jack: Did you know Lake Powell is man-made?

Me: No. Really?

Jack: Yep. Glen Canyon Dam was built across the Colorado River and flooded Glen Canyon.

As I stared up at the sheer cliffs, bright and orange, towering above us against a cloudless blue sky, I couldn't believe it. "Man," it seems to me, is so bad at coming up with truly beautiful things on a grand scale—especially in nature. My mom is forever talking about the Beautiful New Shopping Center, or the Beautiful New Hospital Wing, or that Beautiful New Condo Development, but none of those things seem very beautiful to me. I suppose they are nice in a certain way. I guess the new outdoor mall with the dancing fountains beats the old indoor mall from the eighties with the brown glazed brick and the orange-tile waterfall in the middle that smelled like chlorine and dirty feet.

Still, as I gazed around at the canyon walls I couldn't believe that someone had planned something so perfect and serene, so vibrant and brilliant, full of color and texture and endless sky. Something so . . .

Romantic, isn't it?

(That was Jack.)

I was blown away that he'd said that word just as I was thinking it. I blushed, but I don't think he could tell because my cheeks are a little pink anyway from the sun.

Me (softly): Yeah. It is.

Jack was lying on his back, one hand under his head. I'd been trying not to watch the drops of water that were slowly trickling off his chest and pooling in the little indentations between his abs.

I rolled over onto my back on the raft. The cool water against my legs and the sun warming the wet fabric of the new bikini top stretched across my chest gave me goose bumps. I felt Jack reach out with his free hand and grab my raft, pulling his over. I turned my head to glance at him through my sunglasses but he was staring up at the sky.

We lay there in silence letting the sight of the cliffs against the sky and the heat of the sun on our skin wash over us. There was something electric in the air that I'd never felt before—like someone or something had sucked all the air out of my lungs with a vacuum and I couldn't get a good deep breath.

I realized, floating there under the wide blue sky on rafts tied to the boat, that it was the feeling of anticipation. It felt like something was about to happen.

It felt like something *should* happen.

And then something did.

Jack: They named Lake Powell after John Wesley Powell.

Me: Who was he?

Jack: A one-armed Civil War vet. He explored the Colorado River and this canyon in a wooden boat.

Me: With one arm?

I felt Jack's hand against mine. His fingers were sure and steady as he threaded them through my own. This time when I turned my head, he was looking right at me, a sweet smile on his lips and a twinkle in his blue eyes, as clear and endless as the sky above us.

Jack: Better hold hands while we've still got 'em.

So we did. All afternoon. Even when Jill and Rob came back, Jack didn't let go. Finally, Susan called over the side of the boat from the upper deck and said it was time for us to get cleaned up so we could eat at the marina. We swam to the boat and as Rob and Jill climbed the ladder ahead of us Jack asked if I would be his date to dinner.

I told him yes.

Now I have no idea what to wear. Jill is in the shower and I've dumped both of our bags onto the big bed in our room and I'm trying to find the right top. Thank God Jill told me to bring a skirt. It's a white mini that's perfect for summer—not too short, but looks good with sandals. I got a new top that ties behind my neck. It's the color of a tomato. Jill swears it makes my blue eyes pop. As soon as she gets out of the bathroom I'll wash my hair and survey the sun damage. Hopefully my face isn't too red. I don't want to look like a lobster in this shirt.

I just realized I'm writing about what outfit I'm going to wear. I swear. One cute, sweet guy holds my hand and suddenly, I'm *that* girl. . . .

Whatever. I'm going to let myself be excited. Because I *am*.

I want to not worry about my parents' love life. I want to have one of my own.

Tuesday, June 19
Weight: 126.5

I woke up s-t-a-r-v-i-n-g this morning. No one else was awake yet because we were all up so late last night. (More on that in a moment. But first . . .) I went into the kitchen to get a cup of yogurt. I tried to take small bites and deep breaths in between.

Jill swears that this helps her to eat more slowly. She calls it being "mindful." Apparently the theory is that the food is more satisfying if you are truly aware and conscious of what you're eating instead of just scarfing it down. Which would seem like a good idea, and generally it is. I ate the yogurt slowly and "mindfully" and then drank a bottle of water very "mindfully" and had turned to put the bottle into the recycling bin when I saw the cabinet where Rob and Jack's junk food is stashed. The door was open, and I saw a pack of those little powdered doughnut gems. These doughnuts are my breakfast food kryptonite. I am powerless against their pull. I tore open the cellophane almost before I knew what I was doing and popped one of the tiny powdery doughnuts into my mouth in one bite. I was biting into the second one when I sort of came to. I stood there, frozen, like I had come out of a doughnut gem blackout wondering how I'd gotten here. The doughnut suddenly swelled in my mouth and I saw there was powdered sugar down the front of my sleep shirt. I felt my heart racing as I turned the package over to read the calorie information: 240 calories per serving. Serving size: four doughnuts. That meant every doughnut was sixty calories. Sixty calories in a tiny doughnut I could eat in one bite! The powdered sugar had melted in my mouth and the thick sludge of sweet cake felt like it might choke me if I tried to swallow. I rushed over to the trash can to spit out the doughnut in my mouth. At least I could save an extra sixty calories.

I opened my mouth over the garbage and pushed the mushy clump of calories out with my tongue. I watched the glob tumble from my mouth into the trash bag, and at that exact moment, to my sheer and utter horror, I realized I was not alone. Slowly, I looked up and my eyes met Susan's. I don't know how long Jill's mom had been standing at the counter, but judging from the look on her face, it had been long enough to see me cram a doughnut into my mouth, then check the label on the package and wheel around to spit it out.

There have been several embarrassing moments in my life, but none of them compares in even the smallest of ways with *this* moment. I am unsure how to even write how I felt except to say I wished a hole would open in the boat and I would be sucked to the bottom of the lake and drowned. I would rather have faced death than to have figured out what to say to Susan. Her eyes were sort of wide and I noticed that even this early on the fourth day of a vacation to the lake, her blond hair was thrown up in a twist that *looked* careless and jaunty but was actually planned and perfect. As her gaze drifted from the crumbs on my lips and the white powder dusting my T-shirt to the torn cellophane package in my hand, her perfectly lined lids slowly relaxed into a cool stare.

I straightened up, swiping at my mouth and shirt, trying to dust away the crumbs but only spreading the white confectioner's sugar in a small cloud. I tried to swallow but my mouth was a desert and the longer I stood there in silence the more panicked I became until finally, Susan said, "Well, good morning," and stepped to the counter to make coffee.

I was seized by the urge to make an excuse, to try to find some way to explain why I was covered in sugar and spitting doughnuts into the trash. I felt a fear in the pit of my stomach that didn't make sense. It wasn't a fear that Jill would find out or that Jack would care. It was a fear that I'd disappointed Susan. I folded the cellophane over on the doughnuts and slipped them back into the junk food cabinet and closed the door, then turned to Susan, stammering like a fool.

Me: I . . . I'm just . . . Wow. Those doughnuts are my Achilles' heel.

Susan: Well, we all have our secrets.

Me: Jill has been working so hard, and I want to be a good friend to her. Apparently powdered doughnuts make me a raving lunatic.

Susan: Yes, she would be disappointed, but I won't tell her. Besides. You don't have to worry about being in shape for ballet.

Something about her smile when she said this was like a knife slicing through my chest. It wasn't the extra sixty calories I'd just swallowed that made my stomach hurt, it was the crushing shame of having let Susan down. I was supposed to be a good

71

friend to Jill. I wanted to be pretty enough for Jack. Susan's vision for her son's girlfriend was certainly lean and graceful like her, not wolfing down doughnuts over the trash can. Is this the person I've become? Sneaking bites like my mom? News flash: not a good way to keep a guy interested. If it didn't work for my dad it certainly won't work for a guy as handsome as Jack.

I didn't know what else to say to Susan so I slipped past her to go back to the room I share with Jill. As I did, she turned and stopped me with a hand on my arm.

Susan: You were so beautiful last night. Jack couldn't take his eyes off you. I just wouldn't want you to start forming bad habits that would get in the way of that.

My cheeks were burning, but I forced myself to meet her gaze. This was what tough love must feel like. Susan was telling me the *truth*. She was saying what I *needed* to hear instead of what I *wanted* to hear. Maybe if my mom had a friend like Susan she wouldn't have wound up sobbing into my shoulder while clutching a pint of ice cream. Maybe someone telling her the truth would have kept her from losing my dad.

I nodded at Susan, who smiled at me, then pulled me toward her and kissed my forehead, then poured herself a cup of coffee and asked where my new polka-dot bikini top was hiding.

Susan: Jill couldn't stop talking about what a knockout you

were when you tried it on in the store. I haven't seen it yet!

I smiled and she winked at me as I slipped out of the kitchen and back into my room, where Jill was still asleep. Quietly, I pulled off my sugarcoated T-shirt and fished the polka-dot swimsuit and a little pair of cutoffs from my bag. I also grabbed this journal so I could write about what just happened. I'm sitting in the bathroom on the edge of the tub writing.

It made me feel so good when Jill's mom said Jack couldn't take his eyes off me last night—mainly because I'd felt that too, but I wasn't sure if I was just dreaming. It's nice to have confirmation of good things. Sometimes I get excited about things, and then instantly I feel silly and afraid. This voice in my head tells me that this just *can't* be happening, and that I shouldn't be excited about it because somehow that will jinx it.

Last night Jill and I were getting ready while Rob and Jack helped her dad dock the boat at the marina. When we felt the boat stop and heard the dull roar of the engine go quiet, Jill was changing outfits.

Again.

For the seventh time.

You wouldn't think we'd have had that many outfit changes between us on a trip where we were limited to one bag each.

Let me assure you that this was not the case. We only had three skirts between us, not counting the white one I was wearing. Jill tried on almost every top with almost every skirt.

Me: He's already completely smitten with you. I'm not sure why you're in a panic about what you wear tonight.

Jill (wide-eyed pronouncement face): I am not reacting to panic. I am enacting perfection.

Me: We may miss the appetizers is all I'm saying.

Jill: You can't rush perfection.

Me: No, but you can't eat it either, and if I don't have some food soon, I may lack the strength to actually carry myself down the gangplank under my own power.

At that moment, we heard Susan call for us down the hallway from the stairs that lead out onto the main deck, and Jill took one last look in the mirror before turning and leading the way out of our room, onto the deck, and down the walkway to the dock, where Jack, his parents, and Rob stood waiting. Walking down the ramp, I felt like I was heading to dinner on the dock via a fashion show runway, and as I walked next to Jill, I could sense Jack's eyes on me immediately.

Naturally, Rob couldn't contain himself and let out a low whistle as Jill stepped onto the dock and took his arm. She smiled, then informed him that she was not a baseball game to be whistled at and shot him a look that silenced his joke about getting past third base before it had fully escaped his lips. In the awkward silence that followed, while James glared at Rob and Susan arched an eyebrow at Jill, I felt Jack's hand take mine for the second time that day. He leaned close and whispered into my ear.

Jack: You look great.

Me: I clean up okay.

Jack: Trust me, "okay" isn't the word I would use.

Me: And yet, I received no whistle.

Jack: Not my style.

Me: I like your style.

Jill had not been wrong about dinner: the restaurant was fantastic. The view across the lake was incredible. The sun set as the waiter offered us appetizers, and I caught myself having to ask Jack to repeat himself because I was trying to tally the rough number of calories contained in a small bowl of Southwest corn bisque as compared to the chopped salad. He asked me if I was nervous, and I smiled sheepishly and said maybe a little, even though I wasn't nervous about him, I was nervous about keeping my calories at 1,700 for the day. It dawned on me that I wasn't going to have very much fun if all I did was freak out about calories and lie about being nervous. I decided just to order what Jill was having and not worry about it. Luckily, the waiter went around the table starting with the ladies first in the order we were seated: Susan, Jill, me. Jill ordered the chopped salad to start and something called sixteen-spiced chicken with the mango butter sauce on the side. I followed suit.

Jack and Rob both got the barbecue ribs and Jack insisted I eat one of his, which I did. It was delicious, and I wished I'd gotten that instead of the chicken, but I knew pork ribs are not on a 1,700-calorie diet, so I savored the bite I had and left a little more of the sides on my plate. I kept checking to see if Jill was actually eating. I don't think she took more than a bite or two of her salad, and there was still so much chicken on her plate when the waiter came to offer dessert that her dad insisted he box it up so we could take it back to the boat.

Rob and James both ordered a Lake Powell Brownie Sundae, dripping in caramel and fudge, but Jack opted for the turtle cheesecake. Shockingly, Jill asked for a bite of her brother's dessert and I took one too. I held the rich, creamy bite in my mouth, savoring the combination of the slightly tart cheesecake with the buttery caramel sauce and crunchy graham cracker crust. I didn't realize I'd closed my eyes as I chewed until I opened them and saw Jack licking his fork with his eyebrow raised a little.

Jack: Good, huh?

Me: Transcendent.

Jack (offering another bite): Still hungry?

Me: No, thank you. Stuffed.

I wasn't stuffed, but I felt comfortable again. As I watched Jack place the last mouthful of cheesecake between his perfect lips, I realized I wasn't hungry for food. I was hungry for something else. I blushed when I had the thought, and glanced around quickly, as if I was afraid someone else at the table might've heard my thoughts or read my mind.

When we got back to the boat Jill's dad pulled out of the marina and charted a course for farther out in the lake, where we found a place in a secluded cove to drop anchor and spend the night. Susan seemed especially vigilant about sleeping arrangements after Rob's joke on the way to dinner, so she supervised the Saying of the Good Nights on the upper deck. While Jill made Rob work for a peck on the cheek, Jack smiled at me by the light of the almost-full moon and stuck out his hand toward me as if we were finishing a business meeting in a conference room. I laughed and took it, giving it my firmest pump up and down.

But he didn't let go.

Instead he pulled me in and held our handshake tightly between us while he wrapped his other arm around me in a hug and said, "John Wesley Powell couldn't do this either, poor bastard."

Me: But he did have a wooden boat.

Jack: He had three, actually.

Me: You should stop hugging me now. Your mom is watching.

Jack: She's watching Jill.

Me: She's a wise woman.

Jack: Would you kiss me if she weren't watching right now?

Me: On the first date?

Jack: Yeah.

Me: Not my style.

It took me a long time to fall asleep last night. First, I listened to Jill tell me all about how mortified she was that Rob made that joke, and how she's just not certain if he's mature enough for her. I kept drifting away from what she was saying and thinking about lying on the raft with Jack until finally she said:

Hello?

Me: Sorry. What?

Jill: Wow.

Me: What?

Jill: You've got it bad.

Me: What?

Jill: You've just said "what" three times in a row. You've responded thrice with the word "what."

Me: I was just thinking. . . .

Jill: Yes, yes, about my brother, yes, I know. I am still somewhat dizzy from disbelief.

Me: I think that might be hunger. We didn't eat enough food today to sustain the life of a minnow.

Jill: Might I take this moment to say it is *so* much easier to do this diet *with* someone?

Me: Enjoy it now. I might not survive the boat trip.

Finally, we turned off the light and lay there next to each other in bed. Jill said she wished we could sleep on the upper deck with the guys under the stars. Then she asked me a question.

Jill: So. You and Jack?

Me: Maybe.

Jill: How did this happen?

Me: I don't know exactly. We were lying on the rafts when you and Rob climbed on board this afternoon, and all of a sudden we were holding hands.

Jill: There were no other warning signs? You've known each other for over a decade.

Me: True, but only as your big brother, and me only as your best friend. Generally, every time he saw me at your place I was a sweaty mess after cross-country practice.

Jill just woke up and kicked me out of the bathroom. I can't believe I was in there writing for this long. Sitting on the edge of the tub doesn't feel so good, but I do feel better about the Great Doughnut Gem Incident in the kitchen this morning. Just like folding up socks and T-shirts in my dresser, I know where it goes now. In light of everything else I've written down, it doesn't seem so bad. A few moments of embarrassment, neatly tucked away.

Besides, it was only sixty extra calories. I'll just go easy at lunch.

And no more sneaking food.

I will not turn into my mother.

Wednesday, June 20
Weight: 126

This morning when I woke up, I sneaked into the kitchen and got a cup of yogurt and a bottle of water, then climbed up onto the upper deck. Rob and Jack were already in the water, both of them wearing goggles, swimming laps—sort of. They'd swim out from the boat, then turn around and swim back. Neither of them noticed me until they climbed back up the ladder, laughing and panting. Rob shook his dark curls like a wet dog and I squealed and tried to roll out of the way.

Rob: I'm hitting the shower.

Me: Good luck. I think Jill is in there.

Rob: Maybe I'll join her.

Jack: Dude. I'm standing right here.

Rob: Maybe I'll rephrase.

Me: Maybe you'll bring me another water as penance?

Rob: Anything for you, hot stuff.

Jack: Dude . . .

Rob: I know, I know. You're standing right there.

Rob disappeared down the ladder with his patented hangdog smirk firmly in place, and I laughed while Jack rolled his eyes and ran a hand through his short blond hair. He threw both arms up in the air and turned around slowly, taking in the sights around us once more. The sun glinted off the water droplets that coursed over his shoulders and followed the beautiful curves and divots of the muscles in his back before trickling down the waistband of his board shorts.

That's one thing for sure about this trip: The view never gets old.

(And the lake isn't bad either.)

Later . . .

He kissed me.

It's funny how you think you *know* how certain things are going to happen. I have them all planned out in my head. It's like the movie scripts we worked on last year in English. Mr. DeWalt brought in sample scripts and put us in groups and we each had to adapt a different scene from *To Kill a Mockingbird*. Anyway, we learned about writing the locations and the camera shots and dialogue, and now sometimes I catch myself scripting the things I should say, or wish I'd have said, or hope to get to say.

I was hoping he'd kiss me. Only in the script I had in my head, it was late at night on the upper deck under the big yellow moon, which seems to be getting lower and lower in the sky every evening. It's a waxing gibbous—almost full. (See, Mrs. Brewer? I did learn something in earth science.)

EXT. NIGHT—HOUSEBOAT ON LAKE POWELL

A yellow summer MOON hangs low in the sky, lighting purple cliffs and the eyes of seventeen-year-old JACK, standing at the railing with ME at his elbow.

JACK: It's almost perfect out here.

ME: Almost?

JACK: Yep. It's just . . .

ME: Just what?

JACK: There's too much noise.

ME (*laughing*): Too much noise? It's just us talking.

JACK (*devilish grin*): I know. I have to make that stop.

JACK takes me in his ARMS.

EXT. NIGHT—CONTINUOUS

We push into a CLOSE-UP on JACK and ME kissing, first gently and then passionately, as we PULL OUT and swirl around them, circling them twice, then flying up and away over their heads and the boat zooming out across the water, up the side of the purple cliffs, and fading to white on the MOON.

But that's not how it happened.

We were lying on the rafts again, and Rob had just rolled off his into the water, splashing Jill into a narrow-eyed state of revenge that fueled her attempt to leap onto his head as he swam toward the boat, in an apparent attempt to drown him.

Of course, she weighs 108 pounds (as of this morning), and Rob just continued swimming toward the boat, dragging her along with him, until we were all laughing so hard that if they hadn't reached the ladder, they might actually have drowned in their own mirth. Rob asked Jack if he wanted something to eat and I realized I hadn't eaten since our turkey roll-ups at lunch, but today, I wasn't even hungry.

I realized my body has adjusted to Jill's 1,700 calories and I haven't even thought about it today. I've conquered 1,700 calories! It's almost dinnertime, and I haven't looked at the sun over the cliffs and tried to guess how close we are to being able to eat again, or asked Rob what time it is on his big waterproof watch. As I thought about this, I smiled to myself. Not a big, crazy smile, just a tiny "to myself" smile, and Jack looked at me as I did and he noticed my private smile and he got a tiny smile himself.

EXT. DAY—LAKE POWELL—CONTINUOUS

Camera floats above JACK and ME lying on separate rafts, facing each other.

JACK: What?

ME: Nothing.

JACK: It doesn't look like nothing.

ME: What does it look like?

JACK: I dunno. Like you're . . . happy.

ME: I guess I am.

JACK: When you smile like that it makes me want to kiss you.

ME: Oh, really?

JACK: Yeah, really.

JACK reaches out and pulls my raft closer, then puts one hand on my cheek and leans over and places his lips against mine. He is gentle and his lips taste like ChapStick, warm and smooth against mine. I feel the sun hot on my back, and the water is warm on my legs as I reach out toward his raft, trying to pull him closer to me. I feel his tongue brush against mine, and his breath on my cheek as he tries to adjust into a better angle on his raft, then—

CUT TO WIDE SHOT—EXT. LAKE POWELL—CONTINUOUS

JACK jerks away as his raft slips out from under him. He splashes and thrashes into the water, pulling ME along with him. We laugh and cough, then JACK drapes his arm around his raft and pulls ME close with the other. Suddenly, our legs are tangled up, and my arms are around his broad shoulders, holding on.

ME (*nervous laughing*): Don't want to pull you under.

JACK: You're weightless in the water.

ME (*rolling my eyes*): I am not.

JACK pulls ME even tighter.

JACK (*whispers*): I got you.

JACK kisses ME again. This time we melt into each other and we kiss for a long time, bodies wrapped around each other, his arm pulling me tightly against him.

CAMERA PULLS OUT—LAKE POWELL—CONTINUOUS

Camera pulls away from JACK and ME floating in the clear cool water, pans up the orange canyon walls standing guard around us, and fades into the bright rays of the desert sun.

I guess it wasn't particularly graceful. It wasn't the script I'd written, that's for sure, but when Jack kissed me it was perfect, just as it happened.

I'm ready for the sequel.

Thursday, June 21
Weight: 127

Today was our last full day on the water, and Jill was right
about one thing: her parents got tanked at dinner and were
downstairs in their stateroom by 11 p.m. After her parents
disappeared, Jill snuck downstairs with Rob and came back
with an open bottle of chardonnay they'd left on the counter
and cups for all of us. Dad let me have a sip of wine once
at his brother's wedding, but I'd never been handed a whole
glass.

Rob made a toast about "gorgeous scenery" and "lovely
ladies" and "a week to remember" and Jack laughed and rolled
his eyes, and then held his glass up and looked straight at me.

Jack: To more than friends.

If the moon hadn't been so bright, no one would've seen
me blush, but it was and they did. Rob made a horse sound. Jill
smacked his bare arm. Jack and I laughed, and then we pulled
out the big cushions the guys have been sleeping on all week
and lay down on them and stared up at the stars.

Lying next to Jack on the deck felt different from floating
next to him in the water. He had one hand under his head, and
I used his biceps and shoulder as a pillow. I fit perfectly against

him, my head tucked up under his chin. He felt so sturdy, every inch of him solid and strong. Jill was holding forth on the evils of light pollution and I knew without looking at her that she was wearing her wide-eyed pronouncement face. Then all of a sudden she stopped yammering on midsentence and I glanced over to see Rob kissing her. Jack knew what was happening without looking and groaned that they should get a room. Jill giggled and Rob said "gladly" and they went belowdecks, leaving Jack and me with the sound of the water against the boat.

The stars were so bright out here, and there were so many that the sky looked almost hazy with stripes of twinkling beams. Jack was quiet, and every time he took a breath, I felt his chest rise and fall against my body. It was a different kind of floating, a tide that made me feel like I was drifting closer to him—not physically, but on the inside. Jack must have felt it too, because right at that moment he turned and kissed my hair. He didn't say anything at all, just held his lips there, and he took a deep breath, like he was trying to breathe me in.

The wine was making my head warm, and I felt my heart speed up as I pressed my whole body closer to his. In one slow movement, he rolled toward me and slid his arm under the small of my back, pulling me tightly against him. His lips found mine and he kissed me long and deeply, like he was hungry and he couldn't get enough. I wrapped both arms around his broad shoulders and felt the strength pulsing through his whole body as he held me close. I felt so safe, tucked beneath him, his thick arm wrapped around me, holding on to me like he was drowning in the warmth of my breath and I was the only thing that would keep him afloat.

I slid my hands under the hem of his tank top and let my fingers wander up the knots of muscle in his back and shoulders. He rolled a little to the side, and I felt his hand on my cheek, then it slid down my neck and over my shirt. For a second I was worried. I wished my breasts were bigger and wondered how they felt under his fingers. His touch was firm like the rest of him, but gentle, and suddenly I had goose bumps on my arms. I wanted him to *like* touching me, to *like* the feel of my body as much as I liked the feel of his.

All at once I was so glad that I'd been watching my calories with Jill. I felt lean and pretty under the spell of Jack's hands. I reached up and touched his face, and he moaned softly as his hand found the soft bare skin of my stomach, and he moved his face there, planting tender kisses just above the waist of my shorts, my fingers tangled in his hair.

Right at that second, we heard Jill and Rob laughing on the

stairs. Jack moved back up for a quick kiss on the forehead and whispered one word in my ear:

Damn.

He looked at me with the sweetest smile, his eyes on fire, his cheeks flushed. I winked at him and whispered:

To be continued.

Rob had brought up another half-full bottle of white wine, and we all lay on the cushions laughing and talking and staring at the stars. We must've drifted off to sleep because at some point, Jill was shaking my shoulder and whispering that we had to get back downstairs before her mom got up. The light was gray and purple over the cliffs as I slipped out from underneath Jack's arm and tiptoed back belowdecks to the room I shared with Jill. She fell asleep as soon as we were between the sheets, but I couldn't think about anything but writing all of this down. I have to try to organize what is going on in my head, and inside my heart. I've never kissed a boy like that before. Mom is always saying I have to keep my head on my shoulders and keep boys' hands off to the side. I guess I've always been afraid of not knowing what would happen if a guy actually *did* touch me like that.

There's something about Jack—something I can see in his eyes, and hear in his voice, and feel in his touch—that I know will never hurt me. I wasn't afraid of having him touch me, only that I wouldn't be good enough somehow, and after what happened last night, I'm pretty sure that isn't an issue.

Jill is lying here snoring a little bit and drooling on her pillow a lot, and I'm scribbling in this food diary like a crazy person. I can't even think about closing my eyes. I have this floaty feeling just beneath my chin—almost like a bubble of pure happiness and excitement, mixed with that feeling when you go over the first drop of a roller coaster. I'm not sure I'd call it love. I don't think I've ever been in *love* before. That word seems so . . . serious. Maybe this is what Jill means when she says she's in *lust* with Rob, but I feel like this isn't *just* about Jack having a hot body, or being turned on by him. I think this feeling is probably a crush. It's been growing inside of me since that day at the pool when I first saw Jack as something different from my best friend's brother. It's a feeling that's grown a lot during this week on the boat. It's a feeling I think could grow into love.

I just heard Jill's mom start coffee in the kitchen. We're headed back to the marina this morning. The boat has to be returned by noon, and then we are driving back home this afternoon.

Ugh. Home.

I've barely thought about Mom and Dad and that whole situation since I got here. It makes my stomach hurt. I wonder if

Mom is still crying a lot. You know what? I'm not going to start thinking about it now. I've got one last whole day with Jack, and I'm not going to let myself waste it worrying about how my mom feels.

I'm also not going to let Rob sit next to Jack on the way home.

Sunday, June 24
Weight: 126

Two things were waiting for me when I arrived at home.

1. A shiny new hybrid SUV from my father with more luxury options than I have ever seen on one automobile in my entire life.
2. A shiny-headed, nearly comatose mother, asleep on the couch. I don't think she washed her hair the entire time I was away. She barely moved when I came in the door except when I asked her where the SUV came from.

Mom: Your father.
Me: Why?
Mom (pointing): Note on the counter.

I found a card on the counter, next to a key fob that looked like it might power a spaceship or hold the digital data of a blueprint for the colonization of Mars. In my father's square script were the words:

Want you to be safe on the roads. I know this won't fix things. Maybe it will help.
I love you,
Dad

I stood and stared at the key ring for a full five minutes. The TV was ablaze with a drag queen spatter-painting a bedroom wall, and Mom was staring at it glassy-eyed, not really seeing it. I crumpled the card up and tossed it into the recycling bin, then slipped the key into my pocket and dragged my bag upstairs.

Jack and I sat in the backseat together all the way home. He held my hand, and I fell asleep against his shoulder. I woke up as we drove into town, and the closer we got to my house, the worse my stomach felt. I realized I was dreading walking into the house, and when we'd pulled into the driveway, and I saw the only light coming from the windows was the TV, I knew I'd find Mom asleep in her scrubs on the couch.

It was totally depressing.

Susan gave me a hug in the driveway and told me how glad

she was I'd come with them, and that I was welcome anytime. She made a point of grabbing both of my shoulders and looking right into my eyes and repeating: *Anytime*.

Jack and Rob kept asking where the SUV in the driveway came from, and I kept telling them I didn't know, even though I deep down inside, I knew exactly where it came from. Dad was right. This SUV doesn't fix anything.

But it helps.

I unpacked and went to bed. Yesterday was Saturday, and when I woke up late and Mom was still on the couch, I put my foot down. I made her get up and take a shower. I called the salon we go to and made an appointment, and I dragged her down the stairs to the shiny new SUV, pushed her into the driver's seat, then took her to get a cut, her roots done, and her eyebrows waxed. While she was in the chair, I got a text from Jack.

Jack: Missed you at bfast.

Me: ditto

Jack: whose SUV?

Me: mine ;) peace offering from pop

Jack: NO WAY

Me: way

Jack: I want a ride.

Me: At salon on mayday mission with mom. Call you later.

It was good to get Mom out of the house. She looked

better on the outside after our salon trip and a salad at Lulu's Café across the street. She didn't feel any better on the inside, though. I tried to cheer her up by doing a school-report-worthy rundown of my vacation: My Week at Lake Powell. It was mildly edited. I showed her all the pictures and videos I took with my phone. Rob had brought along these thick plastic zipper bags that sealed tightly, and we took a lot of pictures out on the rafts. I flipped past a couple of Jack and me. I don't want to have to answer questions about him just yet. If I start telling everybody about him, I'm afraid I'll lose that floaty feeling under my chin. I want to keep it all to myself right now.

Mom smiled and halfheartedly munched on her salad, but back at home, she wound up on the couch again for another solid six hours. She was there again when I woke up this morning. All she can do is mope around and talk about how skinny and tan and beautiful I look. It makes me feel sort of frantic on the inside because I want to *do* something about this. It seemed she was doing okay with the whole divorce thing when I left. Now she appears to be falling apart.

I know this is a crappy thing to say about your own mom, but all I could think when I walked in the door on Friday night and saw her sleeping on the couch with greasy hair and dirty scrubs was that Susan would *never* let herself look like that. Ever. She'd go to the guillotine in tailored, matching separates, and her final request would be that someone blot the oil off her forehead so she wouldn't be shiny when she went to meet her maker.

I guess everybody is different.

I'm really glad I had that moment in the kitchen on the boat with the doughnut. It wasn't very fun at the time, but coming back and seeing Mom in this state makes me think it was a good wake-up call when Susan caught me sneaking food. That's how it starts, I think. First you sneak a doughnut, then it's a pint of ice cream, then you're fifteen pounds overweight and your husband is taking somebody else to Korean barbecue.

Monday, June 25
Weight: 126.5

When Vanessa and Geoff showed up to run this morning, they acted like they hadn't seen me since the Paleolithic period. Both of them talked at the same time while we did warm-up stretches. Finally, I just started running because I had to get them winded so only one of them could talk at a time. I thought my run would be horrible because I'd been on the boat for a week, but I think my body actually needed the rest because it felt great to stretch my legs. We decided to time ourselves on a five-mile run, and I couldn't believe it, but I beat Vanessa. I shaved almost a whole minute off my time. They started talking over each other again:

Vanessa: Did you eat anything on that boat?

Me: What? Yes.

Geoff: Your run was awesome, and you look great.

Vanessa: I can't believe it. How'd you manage to lose a couple pounds? You were floating around all day while I was running my butt off.

Geoff: Lighter equals faster!

Of course, that's when Vanessa reminded me we'd have to turn in our printouts from CalorTrack this week at practice. I just looked through my printouts and the numbers are really low. I was kind of surprised at how little Jill and I actually ate. The thing is, I still feel good. Plus, my run today was great. I'll just tell Coach that I cut back because I wasn't running. If she doesn't buy it, I guess I can tell her I'm still not feeling well after the split and everything. If I run as well on Thursday as I did today, she might not be worried about it at all.

Wednesday, June 27
Weight: 126

Mom was working tonight, and Jill called me to see if I wanted to go shopping with her. Jack came into her room while we were talking and this is what I heard:

Jill: What?

Jack: Lemme talk to her.

Jill: What? No. You also own a cell phone. Call her yourself.

Jack: I already did.

Jill: God! You're *hopeless*.

Jill: I've been telling my brother he can't call and text you every five minutes or he'll scare you off. I told him he needs to play it cool. I don't think he really understands the concept.

I was laughing, and I felt my cheeks get warm. Jack and I have been texting like crazy since we got back, and yesterday I drove by in my SUV and took him and Jill for a ride. Since my mom is working most nights, or comatose in front of the TV, I've been going to bed and talking to him before I go to sleep. I'd been sitting on my hands, trying not to call him—to let him make the first move—but it is hard! This feeling I have is more like a roller coaster and less like extreme happiness. Sometimes I think if I don't kiss him again soon, I might disappear in a little puff of white smoke. It made me relieved to know that he was having a hard time not calling and texting more too.

Jill: How did this happen?

Me: What?

Jill: You and Jack?

Me: I don't know. I just . . . saw him at the pool that day.

Jill: I *knew* it.

Me (laughing): What?

Jill: We were walking down that hill toward the car outside the swim club, and I turned around to find Rob. You had your eyes *glued* to Jack. You didn't even hear me when I asked if you wanted to ride with me or Geoff and Vanessa. You just followed us down the hill and climbed into the car with us.

It was true. She was right. That day had changed everything.

Me: Jack and Jill went down the hill . . .

Jill: And you came tumbling after.

Me: (laughing): Something like that.

Jill: You're the worst! You don't even deny it.

Me: Why should I?

Jill: My best friend has the hots for my brother. It goes against the natural order of things.

I could hear her smiling when she said it.

Me: Does that mean I have to choose between you?

Jill: Not if you'll come to the store with me.

She's on her way to pick me up now. I thought she wanted to go to the mall, but she wants to go to Whole Foods. She's got big plans for the next phase of our slim down, which apparently includes a lot of sugar-free gelatin desserts, organic brown rice cakes, dark, leafy greens, and hard-boiled egg whites. It sounds awful.

Jack just texted:

Come by before Jill drops u off. Wanna show you something.

I think I will. Maybe not having Dad at home at nights while Mom is working isn't such a bad idea.

Later . . .

Jill insisted on buying me the same groceries she got for herself. She said she's going to try to get down to 1,000 calories per day this week.

Me: I don't think I can do that.

Jill: Sure you can. You'll actually feel *more* full because these rice cakes totally swell up inside you and fill you up.

Me: Yeah, but I have to run a lot, and Coach is going to expect a lot more calories than I can get from rice cakes and leafy greens.

Jill: So? Just enter extra food. Just because you put it in the app doesn't mean you have to eat it.

This hadn't crossed my mind before. I really like Coach Perkins. She's been so understanding about the whole thing with my dad. I don't really want to lie to her, but my time did get a lot better after I lost a couple pounds. Plus, I know Jill likes having a friend to do this with.

Me: Maybe I can just stay at 1,200 calories.

Jill: Whatever you can do will help. I mean, you saw the

way Jack has gotten hooked on you over the last couple of weeks. What you're doing is working. I wouldn't stop now if I were you.

We pulled into her driveway, and Jack was waiting on the steps. He had this little smirk on his face. Jill took her bag of groceries in and said she was giving us ten minutes and then she was coming back out so we'd better not be steaming up the windows when she did.

Jack grabbed my hand and led me around the house, through the side gate, and into the backyard. My heart was racing the minute he touched my hand. Their backyard has always looked like one of those yards you see on TV shows. The grass around their pool is always perfect and green, and Jack led me down to the double porch swing that hangs at one end of a pergola near the fire pit. He held the swing still while I sat down on it, then he sat next to me and pushed us with his long legs.

I'd been a little nervous when he pulled me into the backyard. For some reason, my mind filled up with the idea that maybe he wanted to make out some more—go further this time. It's crazy what my brain can conjure up when left to its own devices. I had a horrible flash of his dad coming out onto the back steps and finding us practically naked, me scrambling for my bra.

I opened my mouth to say something, but he just said, "Sh!" and pointed up to a giant, round moon that was hanging low in the sky. I hadn't noticed it was full until that moment. He squeezed my hand, and the two of us just sat and stared up at the moon in silence.

As the swing slowed down, my heart sped up and I felt that thickness in the air again.

Me (whispering): Is this what you wanted to show me?

He nodded, then turned and looked at me. He slid one arm around my shoulders over the back of the swing, then reached up with his other hand and pulled my chin toward his. He kissed me once, lightly on the lips.

Jack: C'mon. Let's go say hi to my mom. She won't stop asking me about you.

Me: You showed her that picture on the raft, didn't you?

Jack: How'd you know?

Me: Because I knew my mom would never have let that one go.

He laughed, and my heart jumped at the light in his eyes and the cleft in his chin. Jack is the kind of guy I never had to worry about. This is the boy who wants me to come in and talk to his mom.

He's the boy who wants to show me the moon.

Thursday, June 28
Weight: 125.5

Vanessa is starting to get on my nerves. Ever since Jill and I got back from Lake Powell, she's been asking lots of questions—which is not abnormal or anything, just that they have *all* been on a single subject: eating.

Are you eating enough?

How many calories did you have?

Can I see your CalorTrack printouts?

Ever since we ran on Monday and I had a better five-mile time than she did, she's been all over it. At practice yesterday when we handed in our calorie printouts to Coach Perkins she wanted to compare totals. If Coach noticed I hadn't eaten very much on vacation, she didn't seem to care. She certainly *did* seem to notice when I clocked my best time ever on a five-mile run. We were doing cooldown stretches on the lawn in the big shadow cast by the gym when she walked over, put her hands on my shoulders, and announced my time to the whole team.

Coach: Ladies and gentlemen, *this* is what I'm talking about. Trimming almost a whole minute off a five-mile run isn't easy. It takes determination, and training as much during the summer as you do during the year.

Geoff made a couple of WOOT-WOOTs and then everybody started clapping. Vanessa just sort of looked at me. She was pretty quiet in the car on the way home, and then suggested we stop at Buster's Burgers for lunch.

Geoff: No can do, lovely lady. I'm on a strict budget that I plan to blow on dinner and a movie with you tonight.

Me: Yeah, we're all going out tonight. Let's just eat lunch at home.

Vanessa: I guess. Are Rob and Jill still coming?

Me: Last I heard. I'll text her to confirm.

We pulled into my driveway, and Geoff asked if I wanted a ride over to Jill and Jack's early so we could all leave from their place. I told him I'd just meet them there.

I had a rice cake and half a can of tuna for lunch, along with three full glasses of water, and I almost couldn't finish the last glass of water. I felt stuffed. As I was forcing down the last swallow my phone buzzed.

Jill: What r u doing

Me: Choking down 3rd glass of water

Jill: ATTAGIRL

Me: Rice cakes r tasteless but filling.

Jill: See you soon

I drove over to Jill's about an hour before I was supposed to be there because I was bored, and because I knew she wouldn't care, but mainly because I wanted to see Jack. He had just finished mowing the lawn. He was wearing only a pair of gym shorts, and he was covered in sweat. I parked at the curb and watched him push the lawn mower into the garage, then he turned around and walked down the driveway, his whole body glistening in the sun like somebody had oiled him up.

When I stepped out of the car, he had this mischievous grin on his face, and he came at me like he was going to hug me. I giggled like a total girl and squirmed away, squealing about how he was going to get me all gross.

Get me all gross? It's like I'm in sixth grade again. But you know what? I don't care. Jack makes me laugh.

We went inside, and I talked to Susan for a second. She said I looked fantastic, and I felt really great about my outfit. We were all going to dinner and a movie tonight, and I decided to just keep it casual, but I blew out my hair and put on some mascara and a little bit of eyeliner. I forgot that the whole week on the boat neither of us wore makeup or looked in the mirror much, so it was probably shocking for Susan to see me with eyelashes. Mine are so light that unless I put on mascara they disappear.

Jill called down to me from upstairs, and I followed Jack up to the hallway where her room is. At the top of the stairs, he pecked me on the lips before he went into his room.

Jack: Gonna hit the shower.

Me: Do more than hit it. Go ahead and get into it. Use a little soap.

Jack (smiling): Wanna come with?

Me: Don't make me regret organizing a triple date night.

Jack: This is a date, huh?

Me: That's it. I'm leaving.

He grabbed my hand, held it up to his mouth, and kissed it while he stared into my eyes. I almost fell down. His gaze makes my knees weak.

We both realized that Jill had come to the door of her room when she cleared her throat and we jumped and turned.

Jill: Thank you for that visual. It's as if there is a Disney movie happening in my hallway, only Jack is very sweaty and I think I can smell him from here.

Jack ran down the hall toward her with his arm raised, shouting at her to get a good whiff, while she ran shrieking into her bedroom and slammed the door. I was laughing when he passed me in the hall and paused.

Jack: You look beautiful tonight.

Me: You're not so bad-looking yourself.

Jack: And in a minute, I'll smell good enough to eat.

Me: Hurry up. I'm hungry.

He winked and headed into his bedroom. I watched him go,

then sighed and walked down the hall to Jill's room. I watched her try on fourteen different tops and T-shirts of a startling variety. She finally settled on the first one she had modeled for me some twenty minutes prior, then spent another five minutes picking out summer sweaters for both of us. We live in a place where summers are hot and dry, but even though it's still in the eighties after the sun goes down, Jill has an intense fear of being too cold in movie theaters. By the time she'd chosen outfit-appropriate sweaters for each of us, Geoff and Vanessa were in the driveway.

At dinner, Vanessa was on a mission about food:

Is that all you're ordering?

You ran like twenty miles this week.

Just a salad?

You didn't even finish it all.

Her obsession with what I was eating was so pointed even the guys started noticing her comments. Geoff looked really uncomfortable, and Rob smirked as he asked if she'd like to cook for us all next time, that way she could make sure we were all eating the right thing. Jill finally silenced her with an icy gaze and a firm tone while explaining that she and I were saving room for treats during the movie. This made Vanessa stop commenting, but also made her stop talking, and the rest of dinner was very strange. I saw Geoff slip his arm around her and squeeze her shoulder, and suddenly I felt really guilty. I could still sense Vanessa's eyes on me every time I took a bite, and again when I told the waiter he could take my plate.

Thankfully, Vanessa and Geoff had driven separately, and I'd been elected earlier by a show of hands to drive Rob, Jill, and Jack in my new car. The heady smell of new interior leather filled our nostrils, while Jack opened the sunroof and played DJ with my phone, which is synched via Bluetooth to the stereo system. By the time we arrived at the theater, the weirdness with Vanessa had been momentarily forgotten, and when we met her and Geoff at the ticket counter, she came with Jill and me to the bathroom, where we touched up lip gloss while Jack, Rob, and Geoff got tickets.

Jill and Vanessa and I stood in front of the mirror for a minute and laughed as Vanessa wondered aloud about the movie. How we'd gotten ourselves roped into seeing a blockbuster about killer alien robots disguising themselves as United States congressmen and the heroic Capitol Hill page who uncovers their plot to take over the planet I'll never be quite sure, but I have a feeling Rob's calves, Jack's eyes, and Geoff's grin had something to do with it. Somehow, the tension from dinner melted away in the bathroom and I thought maybe we'd get through the night without any more weirdness about calorie counting from Vanessa.

Then we met the guys in the line for concessions.

Rob and Jack ordered popcorn and large Cokes. The cups were so gigantic they appeared to be small barrels with straws. Rob wanted black licorice bites and Jill told him that he should under no circumstances expect her to kiss him if he ate black licorice bites all night, so he settled for Goobers. He also told Jill that *she* was a Goober, which she said was disgusting, and then he asked if she wanted anything. Jill and I had agreed to just get bottles of water because she had rice cakes in her purse for us to munch on. So we both got our water, and the guys balanced gigantic buckets of popcorn.

I should note that Jill carries an enormous designer purse she received from her mother for Christmas last year. In addition to being very stylish, it is large enough to hold a bicycle and still carry an immense amount of personal belongings. When we got to our seats, Jill opened her purse and pulled out a couple of rice cakes in a Baggie and our stylish summer sweaters, handing one of each to me.

Vanessa was sitting on the other side of Jack, next to Geoff, eating popcorn, and made a noise like a car backfiring.

Jill: What?

Vanessa: Those are your treats?

Jill: Indeed. These are the aforementioned treats. Do they not meet with the approval of the treat police?

Vanessa just looked at me and shook her head. Mercifully, at that moment the lights went down and the previews started. Jack leaned over and whispered in my ear.

Jack: What's up with her?

Me: She thinks we're not eating enough.

He held out the popcorn bucket.

Me (laughing): No. But I want a Junior Mint.

Jack grabbed the box before I could reach for it and placed it protectively on the other side of the popcorn.

Jack: No. We can't open the candy until the actual movie starts.

Me: Says who?

Jack: It's my movie candy rule. Otherwise, it's all gone before the movie starts.

Jill (not whispering): SHH.

About the time the incredibly buff, young Senate page discovered the body of his boss had been inhabited by an alien robot who was headed to the White House for a "meeting" with the president, I got really cold and pulled on the sweater Jill had loaned me. Jack folded up the armrest between us and I snuggled into him. He put his left arm around me and I could feel his heart beating in his chest against my shoulder.

As the Senate page led a Special Forces contingent to a final battle against the alien robots on the stairs of the Lincoln

Memorial, he was wearing only a white tank top that had been revealed when his suit and tie were blown off in an explosion. Instead of rolling my eyes, I smiled to myself. Sitting there with Jack, feeling the rise and fall of his chest, the warmth of his arm around me, I felt like I was starring in my own movie, and nothing could wipe the smile off my face.

Afterward, we all went back to Jack and Jill's, where Susan and James were polishing off a bottle of wine and insisted we all come in. Jill pulled a container of sugar-free gelatin out of the fridge while James scooped massive bowls of ice cream. The Jell-O was strawberry flavored and Jill had cut it into star shapes with a cookie cutter. It was cold and delicious and, best of all, calorie free.

We all went outside to the backyard, and while Rob and Jack ate ice cream and debated baseball standings with Geoff, I kicked off my sandals and sat down on the edge of the pool with my bowl of strawberry stars. The water felt cool, then warm, against my legs. Vanessa came over and joined me, rolling up her jeans, then sitting next to me with her bowl of chocolate ice cream. She told me she was sorry about earlier and that she was worried that I wasn't going to get enough calories for the week.

I told her not to worry, that I was keeping track of it. I said that I eat like a horse at home during the day and was just trying not to eat as much around Jill because she's working so hard on her ballet body. I told her everything she wanted to hear, and when Geoff looked at his watch and said he had to get home, Vanessa gave me a hug and all was forgiven.

I finished my Jell-O, but it didn't taste as good as it had before Vanessa sat down. Maybe it was because her chocolate ice cream looked so delicious. Or maybe it was because I'd just lied to my friend. I *am* keeping track of it. That part was true.

I took my bowl back into the kitchen and laid Jill's sweater on the counter, then told everybody I was tired. My stomach felt strange. Maybe it was the bizarre combination of food: half a salad, rice cakes, and Jell-O on top of the three Junior Mints I'd allowed myself during the movie. James and Susan both gave me a hug. Jill said she'd text me tomorrow. Jack walked me to my awesome/ridiculous new car and leaned against the driver's-side door.

Me: I need to get in there.

Jack: I'm going to need a kiss first.

Me: What if your mom is watching from the living room window?

Jack: Then she's going to see us kiss.

I just got home. Mom is working until 2 a.m., so it's quiet here, but my heart is still racing a little bit. When Jack kisses me it makes me breathless like I just ran for a mile. It's nice to feel like that, but sometimes, it's also a little tiring. After the past three weeks, between Dad leaving and vacation and Jack and this whole thing with Vanessa, I just feel really tired. ~~I'm going to take a long, hot bath and then~~

Jack just texted me. He left his wallet in my car. He's driving over to get it. My heart is racing. Seeing him again is better than a long, hot bath anyway.

Later . . .

Jack just left.

I met him in the driveway and unlocked my SUV. He climbed in and found his wallet wedged down by the seat belt in the passenger seat. When he got out, he looked up at my house.

Jack: So, this is where you sleep?

Me: Not so far tonight.

Jack: I wanna see.

Me: Me sleep?

Jack: That too.

I took his hand and led him up to the front porch. The sprinklers were *phrip-phrip-phripping* water all over the yard, and my bare feet got wet as we ran between them. When we walked through the front door, I told him I was breaking the rules.

Jack: What rules?

Me: No boys in the house when there isn't an adult present.

Jack: I turn eighteen in October. Does that count?

Me: No.

Jack: I guess I should go.

Me: No.

Jack: You'd break the rules for me?

Me: Just a little. Mom gets off in an hour.

I gave him the grand tour but didn't linger here in my bedroom, even when he sat down on the bed. Something about it felt like it was too much. We went back downstairs to the kitchen. I got him a Coke and a Diet Coke for myself, and we carried them into the living room and sat down on the sectional.

I leaned over his legs to grab the remote, and he wrapped his arms around me, then lay back on the couch, easily swinging me on top of him. Then we were kissing, and the remote and the Cokes were forgotten. It was like we were right back on the deck of the boat at Lake Powell, only this time my shirt came off too. When it did, he took a deep breath and lay back as his hands gently caressed my arms and chest. The only light was from the moon, leaking in through the window. It turned our skin a pale blue in the dark living room, and as he pulled my face gently back toward his lips, he breathed, "You are so beautiful."

Who knows what other articles of clothing might have come off if I hadn't had the sound turned up on my phone and heard the text message?

Mom: Headed home now. Need anything?

Me: No thanks. Sleepy. C u in a.m.

Jack rolled over on his stomach while I texted her back, and lay there for a second while I put my T-shirt back on.

Jack: I have to go home now, don't I?

Me: Well, you don't *have* to, but if you don't, my mother may kill me while you watch when she returns.

Jack: I'd never forgive myself.

Me: Then you might want to think about putting on your shirt.

He pulled his T-shirt on in a hurry and sort of tugged the hem down past the waist of his shorts.

Me (laughing): Little riled up, are we?

Jack: Hey, that's *your* fault.

Me: I will not stand for these wild allegations.

He put an arm around my shoulders as I walked him to the front door and we stepped out onto the porch.

Jack: Thanks for the tour.

Me: Thanks for coming by. Didn't know I'd see you again tonight.

Jack: I did.

Me (frowning): Really?

Jack: Whydaya think I left my wallet in your car?

Then a kiss, and a wink, and he was gone.

Saturday, June 30
Weight: Can't look yet.

The only thing missing from my birthday last night was Dad.

It's strange, but I can't remember a birthday without him. Because my birthday is never during school, he'd always take the day off from work at the dealership so we could have the whole day together. Every year for as long as I can remember, he always made chocolate chip pancakes for breakfast. He'd drop the chocolate chips in after he'd poured the batter to arrange them in the numbers of whatever birthday it was.

Yesterday was sixteen. But no chocolate chips—just a text from Dad:

HAPPY BDAY! Call me when you can. XO

I haven't talked to him yet. I feel guilty about it. I should at least call him and thank him for the car, but I haven't done it yet. Every time I think I'm ready to, Mom traipses into the kitchen looking like a zombie, and it makes me angry on the inside. Not burn-down-a-building angry. It makes me just angry enough to put down my phone.

Dad was always the one up and at 'em on weekend mornings. He liked to go to the gym before he went to the dealership. He was usually back making breakfast by the time I woke up on Saturdays and because Mom usually works Friday nights, it was just him and me eating omelets and talking on Saturday mornings.

When I got his text yesterday morning, I was lying in bed, listening to the silence of Mom sleeping late. My heart started pounding in this weird way, like I was going to be in trouble or something. I poised my thumbs over the screen to tap a message back to him, but I didn't know what to say, and I realized I was holding my breath.

I took in several long, deep breaths like I do when I find my rhythm running. It helped my heart to stop pounding so hard, and I sent him a little smiley face back:

=)

Maybe it's a start.

I didn't have high hopes for my birthday last night, but Mom managed to surprise me. Not only did she take Friday night off, she was dressed and looking nice when I got back from my afternoon run with Vanessa and Geoff. To top it all off she sprang a surprise on me. She'd called the whole gang and invited everyone over for taco night. She had a gigantic devil's food cake in the oven, and the whole house smelled so good my head got sort of light and loopy. I realized while I was standing in the kitchen with Vanessa and Geoff that I hadn't had a single bite of anything cakelike since that doughnut Jill's mom caught me eating on the boat. I made a decision right then and there that I was going to enjoy my birthday, and just not care about the calories for one day.

Vanessa and Geoff arrived at the same time that Jill and Rob showed up. Jack appeared on the front steps about five minutes later with a fistful of flowers. They were long-stemmed red roses, so bright and beautiful that they took my breath away. Let me stop here and say that I've only seen men arrive with flowers in movies. I've been trying to remember a time when my dad arrived at the door with flowers for my mom or me and I simply can't. Typically, when he showed up with a surprise, it was a car of some kind. As I stared at Jack's blue eyes, twinkling over the tops of the roses, I decided that flowers were better than an SUV any day.

Mom's tacos are delicious. They always are. There's something about the way she seasons the meat that knocks them out of the park. Everybody but Jill loaded up a big plateful. Jill took half a spoonful of ground beef and a sprinkling of shredded lettuce. Mom and the boys were back in the living room plugging the old video camera into the television so that my annual birthday humiliation of watching videos of myself as an infant could commence. I'd almost made it across the kitchen to where the great room becomes the living room on the other side of the island when I heard it:

Vanessa (to Jill): Is that really all you're going to eat?

Jill (quietly): That's your limit.

Vanessa: What?

Jill: You get one comment about what I'm eating tonight, Vanessa, and that was it.

Vanessa: I just want to make sure that—

Jill: Mind. Your. Own. Business.

I kept walking. Jill can hold her own.

I had a headache and a stomachache this morning when I woke up. I think it was all the sugar and calories. I had three tacos and two pieces of cake last night. It was so good, I felt like I was high. Or what I imagine it might feel like to be high. I've never smoked anything in my life.

Later . . .
Weight: 126.5

I just got on the scale in Mom's bathroom.

Mayday.

I was still at 125.5 on Thursday. Then I ran yesterday. I gained a full pound overnight, just from that crappy birthday cake and those damn tacos.

Mom was downstairs making coffee when I went into the kitchen earlier, and she was all chipper and smiling and asking if I wanted to try on the new outfit she bought me. She even wanted to make me breakfast. I poured a mug of coffee and told her I had to wake up before I could eat anything else. The cake was still

118

sitting out, and she lifted up the tinfoil and swiped a little chunk of it off the side of the plate. Watching her lick the fudge frosting off her fingers almost made me throw up. I sort of wish I had. What was I thinking last night? I ate like I was going to the electric chair.

The worst part is that I know I let Jill down. She was *so disciplined* and didn't eat a single bite of cake, but still seemed to be having a great time with the rest of us. That's just it: I still think I *need* to eat food to be having fun with everyone else. The truth is, I don't want to be like everyone else. I want to be different. The reason Jack likes me is not because I look like every other girl; it's because I look *different* from any other girl.

Last night, everybody else left around midnight, and I walked him outside to his car. He leaned over and kissed me for a long time, then told me I was different from any girl he'd ever gone out with before.

I intend to stay that way.

As soon as Mom left, I took the cake and dumped it into the kitchen trash can, then hauled the trash bag outside and tossed it into the garbage can on the side of the garage. I don't need to have that in the house. And Mom *certainly* doesn't need to be sneaking bites from it all day and night. She'll end up eating the whole thing, and more devil's food on her thighs is *not* what she needs right now.

My head is pounding. I feel bloated. This is the price I pay for not sticking to my guns yesterday. I'm so stupid. I *know* better than this. I could see it in Jill's eyes when I got the second slice of cake and was licking the frosting off my fork. She gave me this little smile, this sad little smile as if she was saying, are you sure this is worth it?

The answer is *no*.

Nothing is worth feeling like this. There are far better feelings in the world: Jack's eyes on me as I cross the room. His hands on my body as I slide off his shirt. His lips on mine, breathing me in. Beating Vanessa by a full minute on a five-mile run.

Run.

That's what I need to do right this minute.

Run.

Sunday, July 1
Weight: 126

I feel so much better tonight. I ran seven miles yesterday, and Jill texted me while I was out. I called her after my run, and started crying on the phone about how I'd messed everything up, and lost control, and told her I was sorry for letting her down. I don't know how she does it, but Jill is one of the most completely calm people I know—especially when someone else is having a breakdown. She's in control *all the time*.

Jill: It's not a problem. You didn't let me down.

Me: I just don't want to end up fat and unhappy like my mom.

Jill: Not a chance.

Me: How do you know?

Jill: Because you called me crying about eating your own birthday cake.

Me: I threw the rest in the trash and ran seven miles just now.

Jill (laughing): See? Take a deep breath and meet me at the park.

So I did.

Jill showed me this aerobic workout she does that you can do anywhere. It's just isometric exercises mainly that give you some resistance training using your own body weight while also getting your heart rate up. It kicked my butt. She explained that if you do it correctly, it burns three hundred calories in twenty-five minutes. Anytime she feels like she's overdone it foodwise, she does this in her room, or jogs down to the park and does it outside, here in the grass.

Afterward, we went back to her place and lay by the pool for a while. Jack and his dad came home from a bike ride while we were out there. I heard a low whistle and when I turned around, Jack was standing there in these little spandex bike shorts and his cycling shoes. He kicked off the shoes and pulled off the helmet and his jersey, flinging sweat all over the place, then did a cannonball off the side of the pool and got us completely soaked. Jill calmly blinked the water out of her eyes and blotted her face with a heavy sigh while I shrieked.

Jill: Your boyfriend is so charming.

Me: And the only guy I've ever seen who looks sexy in bike shorts.

Jill: I'm going to pretend you didn't say that.

Tuesday, July 3
Weight: 125

If Vanessa asks me if I'm "okay" one more time, I'm going to implode. She just left, and all she could talk about was making sure that I'm getting enough calories so I don't lose any more weight, because if I do Coach is going to start to notice. The thing is, I've only lost eight pounds since we started keeping track. That's not too much. It's perfect. When I look in the mirror, I don't see baby fat covered in acne anymore. I see a face that looks more grown-up. (Pretty, even? I think Jack is convinced of that . . . I wonder if I'm really . . . pretty?)

I feel like I've finally mastered how to stay in shape and look the way I want to. After suffering through Mom convincing me to cut my hair off in seventh grade (huge. mistake.) and then zits on my forehead and nose like fireworks until she finally took me to the dermatologist in ninth grade, it's like I've come to a place where I'm not at war with my body anymore. It's like I've taken control of the way I look.

My phone just rang again.

It's Dad.

Again.

Every time I see his name flash up on the screen it makes my stomach hurt. He keeps leaving messages about coming to watch fireworks with him on July 4th. Mom has to work that night, so I guess I could, but I don't really want to see him yet. I don't know what to say. I know I have to talk to him at some point.

I can't just ignore him forever.

Friday, July 6
Weight: 124.5

I just got back from practice, and I want to strangle Vanessa. She's been great all week. She and Geoff and I have been running almost every day in the mornings. After we get back, Vanessa goes to babysit her nieces most days, and Geoff is working construction with his dad. So in the afternoons, Jill and I jog down to the park and do the workout she showed me, then we go back to her place and lay out by the pool.

Jill is still keeping her calories down to about 1,000 per day, and I'm doing around 1,200 or so. It's not that hard, and I feel full most of the time. I have two hard-boiled eggs for breakfast, a rice cake snack after we get back from running, and then a salad for lunch, and another salad for dinner, usually with a little chicken or tuna fish on it. Of course, I drink about twenty glasses of water every day, and I keep a couple bags of gummy fruit snacks in my bedside table. I let myself have one or two a day just to keep from going crazy. But it's not hard, and I can't believe how great I look in the mirror. I love my new body. I look like those girls in the workout ads for yoga clothes and running shoes. The other day when we were swimming, Jack said my six-pack was better than his. This is patently false; Jack has washboard abs like one of those European soccer stars in underwear commercials, but it made me smile and blush, so of course, I splashed him in the face so he wouldn't see how happy it made me, and he dove at me and knocked me off my raft.

Jill looks so thin her legs don't touch between her thighs anymore. I don't really understand the rules of how you have to look in ballet, but she tells me that it's all about being as light as possible so you can be lifted, and almost weightless in your jumps and spins. If "almost weightless" is the standard, Jill should have no trouble getting the roles she wants next week when her summer ballet intensives start. If she gets any more weightless, she'll float away.

All of this would be fine and good except that today at practice when we handed our CalorTrack printouts in to Coach Perkins, Vanessa lost her mind again. Coach glanced down at my sheets, then smiled and patted me on the back and told me I was doing a great job. I've been putting in a few extra things on the CalorTrack app that I don't actually eat, but nothing major. Just adding some toast to the eggs at breakfast and a turkey sandwich to the salad. Sometimes a brownie or some frozen yogurt for "dessert" after dinner. I don't do it for every day or anything—just enough to up the calories for the week by about 750 or so.

Vanessa heard Coach tell me I was doing a great job, and I heard her sigh really loudly like hearing this was *just so taxing* she simply *couldn't endure*. I shot her a dirty look, maybe a little dirtier than I should have, and she rolled her eyes. I'd ridden with her and Geoff, so after practice I was just completely silent in the car. Finally, she turned around and asked me what my problem was.

Me: No problem, Vanessa. None at all.

Vanessa: Right. Except for that look you shot me, and now you're not talking.

Me: You're the one sighing like there's a foreign missile crisis every time Coach tells me I'm doing a good job.

Vanessa: And you're the one *lying* about how much you're eating.

Me: Vanessa, do you see everything I put in my mouth each day?

Vanessa: All I know is that—

Me: Didn't ask what you *know*. Asked if you see everything I put in my mouth each day.

Geoff: Hey, you guys. Chill out. It's not that big a—

Vanessa and me: Shut up, Geoff.

Me: I'm eating plenty. I'm running better than I ever have. You're just jealous because you're not beating me in the five-mile anymore.

Vanessa: Oh. Yeah. That's it. You are such a liar.

Me: What?

Vanessa: You heard me.

I got out of the car and slammed the door. Geoff jumped like he'd been shot at. I was so mad I had to come straight upstairs and write about it. I'm sick of Vanessa's attitude. I look great, I feel great, I've got a great body and a great boyfriend, and she can't handle it because I'm beating her. Some friend. When she and Geoff started going out last year, I was so happy for her. I've been riding around as their third wheel for months now, and all of a sudden when things start to go well for me, she has to get all hot and bothered about it.

Screw her.

I don't need that noise.

Thank God for Jill. She's the only one who understands me. I'm going over there for dinner tonight. Rob is staying there this weekend while his parents are out of town for their anniversary. We're going to have a big cookout. Jill didn't tell Vanessa and Geoff. I'm glad. I don't think I could possibly deal with any more judgment from that direction this evening.

Monday, July 9
Weight: 124

Mom had the day off from work yesterday. When I woke up it was weird because I actually smelled coffee and bacon cooking. For a minute, I was confused because I imagined that Dad was downstairs making breakfast, and before I was really fully awake, I felt this funny excitement and actually smiled, and snuggled down into my pillows under my comforter, waiting for him to rap on the door and tell me the waffles or the omelets were ready.

Then it hit me: Dad doesn't live here.

My eyes flew open, and suddenly I was awake, and I had this strange sinking feeling. It was like I'd forgotten I was mad at Dad, and it made me feel stupid and sad at the same time;

stupid because I can't let him off the hook that easily, and sad because . . .

(Why is it so hard to even write this down?)

Sad because I miss him.

There. I said it. I miss him. I wish he'd been nicer to Mom. I wish they could have worked it out. When I was over at Jack and Jill's the other night having the cookout with Rob and these neighbors of theirs from next door, I couldn't help noticing how easy Susan and James were with each other. It's not that they don't ever have little "moments" where they disagree. It's just that they're nice to each other about it. It seems like they rarely have those "moments" at the same time. I saw Susan get briefly frustrated when James set down a knife he'd used to cut up some raw chicken on her clean cutting board, but instead of snapping at him about it, she glanced around the room and just asked him to rinse off that knife. It was a small thing, but it was such a big thing. My dad would've cursed under his breath and grabbed the knife and tossed it into the sink or something. Then Mom would've looked extra hurt and been crazily apologetic and scurried around trying to "fix" things and overcompensated, which would have annoyed Dad even more until he finally snapped at her to get out of his way. I saw that happen a lot between them, and it didn't matter who was around.

Anyway, I went downstairs and was thinking about all of

this and was surprised to see Mom sitting there with coffee and . . . bacon. No eggs. No waffles. Just a big plate of bacon.

Mom: Good morning, honey.

Me: That's a lot of bacon.

Mom: Want some?

Me: Not really the breakfast of champions.

Mom (moaning): I *know*. I just needed a little pick-me-up.

Me: Have you been exercising at all? You know working out fires up the feel-good in your brain.

Mom (sighing): I know. I just . . . I don't know how you do it. I'm so old, and I have no energy, and . . .

Her voice trailed off, and she popped another piece of bacon into her mouth. I ate a couple of hard-boiled eggs and drank a glass of water and a cup of coffee. When I was done, I rinsed out my mug and put it into the dishwasher. Then I picked up her plate of bacon and put it on the counter next to the sink.

Me: C'mon.

Mom: Hey! What?

Me: Put on your tennis shoes and some workout shorts.

Mom: What? Why?

Me: We're going to go for a jog.

Mom: Oh . . . no. Honey. I can't jog.

Me: How do you know?

Mom: I just haven't in like . . .

Me: Now. We're leaving in five minutes.

I couldn't actually believe it, but when I came back downstairs, she was lacing up her old running shoes.

The whole attempt was disastrous, naturally. We jogged down the block toward the park and had to walk the next block. Then I made her jog again. We did this all the way there, and the more she stopped and whined about how she was having a hard time breathing, or her ankles hurt, or her knee felt funny, the angrier I got. When we finally got to the park, I walked her over to the workout stations where Jill and I do sit-ups and push-ups, and dips and showed her how to start. I sat at her feet and she did four sit-ups before she lay back on the wooden bench huffing and puffing and said, I can't!

Me: Yes, you can.

Mom: Honey, you don't understand.

Me: Yes. I *do* understand. I understand perfectly. I understand that you don't care enough about yourself to take care of yourself. You don't care enough about me to take care of yourself. And you *certainly* didn't care enough about *Dad* to take care of yourself.

I didn't realize I was crying until I saw that she was crying too. I stood up and took off running across the park. I ran down the street, then turned away from our house and ran toward the mountain. I ran until the tears had stopped, which must've been at least four miles, then I turned around and ran toward home.

When I got here, Mom's car was gone. She'd left a note that she'd gone out with her girlfriend Pam. Pam is Mom's truly overweight friend from the hospital. They've worked nights together in the ER for years. Mom might have twenty pounds to lose. Pam is obese. She has big sacks of fat that wiggle on her arms, making her elbows just dimples from behind. She's always wearing sleeveless tops for some reason. Probably because sleeves on her arms look like sausage casings about to explode.

In the shower, I could just picture them sitting at Pam's favorite restaurant, this sports bar called Dick's Hot Wing Express. I could smell the buffalo sauce dripping off Pam's greasy fingers while she poured more light beer for my mom and listened as Mom cried and talked about how hard this has all been on her.

After my shower, I opened my drawer and realized I was almost out of clean clothes. I went down to the laundry room, and there was a load of whites just sitting in the washer, soaking wet. They'd been there overnight, so I set the machine to rinse again, and as I marched back upstairs, I saw the empty bacon plate sitting on the counter. Mom had eaten the rest of it when she got back, I guess. Something about that made me so angry, I wanted to throw it across the kitchen. Instead, I ran over to the couch and picked up a throw pillow off the floor and hit the couch with it over and over again. The living room was a wreck of Mom's dirty dishes and old newspapers, books, and ice cream bar wrappers. I thought about Jill's place. It was always gorgeous. It looked like a page out of a catalog for a furniture store—like Susan had styled the whole place.

Mom is still in bed this morning, but last night, I decided several things:

1. I'm getting a job. Now that Jill has ballet intensives for the next month, I can't stand being here with Mom all the time.
2. This wasn't all Dad's fault. I feel like since he's been gone, I'm seeing the things that must have driven him crazy about Mom. Maybe I'll call him this week.

Wednesday, July 18
Weight: 122

Turns out it's not as hard to get a job as I thought it would be.

On Saturday, Jill and I went to the Springs, which sounds like the name of a spa but is actually this big outdoor shopping mall near our neighborhood. They built the place around a big computerized fountain that squirts water in the air synchronized to music, then it splashes down and is pumped through the whole mall in little troughs along the walkways. It's sort of nice until you realize that there isn't a single blade of grass anywhere except for two strips in the medians near the parking deck. The entire shopping center is a giant slab of concrete.

Jill had to get new tights and toe blocks before she started ballet intensives on Monday, and while she was in the dance supply store, I noticed a Help Wanted sign in the window at this big chain Italian restaurant across the walkway called Parmesan's. I got an application and the hostess on duty explained that you start as a food runner, and then if it goes well, after a month or so they promote you to hostess. The pay isn't so great—minimum wage, but you do get "tipped out" by the waiters after every shift, and in my book, it seems that *not very good* still beats *nothing at all*. So I was happy when Melanie, the manager, called me in for an interview on Monday.

Melanie is tall and very excited about her role in management at Parmesan's, a member of the Brighton Restaurants LLC family, owned by Farnsworth Food Services Group. She asked me a number of the most high-energy, ridiculous questions I have ever heard regarding my strengths, my weaknesses, my overall level of commitment, and my goals in life. I am happy to report that I smiled and nodded and gave the Correct Answer each time. By the end of the interview you'd have thought I had only ever envisioned for myself a career in running bottomless bowls of salads and baskets of breadsticks to the lunch crowd here at the Springs location of Parmesan's. Satisfied with my enthusiasm, and after commenting on my clean fingernails and hair, Melanie offered me two starched white aprons, a photocopy of the Parmesan's uniform requirements and a firm handshake. I was hired on the spot.

My first shift was on Tuesday. Melanie explained that I'd work lunches until I proved I could handle a dinner rush, and filled me in on the Brighton Restaurant laws:

1. A smile on the face equals joy on the plate.
2. Full hands in, full hands out. (Of the kitchen.)
3. No questions asked.

When I first started, I was really nervous, but I just kept a big smile on my face and followed around this other runner named Angela. She showed me how to pop fresh breadsticks into the warmer and make sure they were smothered in butter and garlic salt before we loaded them into baskets. The salad bowls are premixed by the guys on the salad line, but then we have to pour the dressing on and toss it at the table. I'm also responsible for running around with water and iced tea pitchers, and Angela showed me how to approach the tables and serve plates over the person's left shoulder and clear from the right. In that sense the service flows like you'd read a book in English—from left to right. Serve to the left, clear from the right. I was worried I might drop something, or spill something, but I didn't. I did accidentally try to clear a salad bowl that had a single leaf of lettuce in it and looked empty to me. The woman at the table nearly fell out of her chair, covering the bowl with both hands:

Her: *No!* I'm not finished with that!

Me: Oh! I'm so sorry.

I blushed really hard, but I kept a big Parmesan's Team Smile on my face and picked up an armload of other dirty dishes from the table so that I could go back into the kitchen. That's what full hands in, full hands out means: on the way in I have to be carrying dirty dishes to the dish room, and on the way out I have to be carrying clean dishes full of food.

Andy was the waiter at that table, a smiley college guy who was studying premed. He spotted me refilling two more breadstick baskets for that table a few minutes later and told me not to worry about it.

Andy: I don't know where she put that extra bite of salad.

Me: Probably the same place she's going to put these two baskets of breadsticks.

Andy (laughing): I should check her purse.

Me: She'd try to stop you, but I think she's stuck in her chair.

As I carried the breadsticks and a fifth glass of Diet Coke to this table, I looked around and really noticed who was eating in this restaurant. Almost every single person was overweight except for the waiters. There were four women at Andy's table including the one whose salad I'd tried to clear, and each one of them seemed to spill over the arms of her chair. Suddenly, a wave of nausea swept over me. The smell of the butter and garlic on the breadsticks turned my stomach. I will *never* look like these people. I heard Susan's voice echo in my head. One night on the lake she'd watched with an approving grin as Jill refused a bite of Rob's dessert, and said something that now made total sense to me:

Nothing tastes as good as thin feels.

For the rest of the shift, those words rang in my ears. I picked up the pace while I walked around looking for dishes. I realized my new job is almost all exercise! I'm going to buy a pedometer to see how far I actually walk during a shift. I'm burning calories the whole time.

Later, Angela and I helped Andy carry out the entrées for his table. Each of these women had ordered a heaping plate of fettucini with creamy Alfredo sauce. As Angela and I slid the plates onto the table in front of each guest, Andy leaned over the shoulder of the woman who had panicked when I tried to take her salad with a grater and a block of cheese.

Andy: Fresh Parmesan?

Her: Oh my, yes! (conspiratorially to her friend) Hard cheese is on my diet.

When she said this, I almost laughed out loud. Instead, I bit my tongue until it almost bled and finished picking up the empty bread baskets that littered the table. One of the other women saw my big grin and commented that I had the prettiest smile she'd ever seen.

Andy followed me back into the kitchen and we stood at the dish stand and laughed.

Andy: Her *diet*?

Me: I *know*!

Andy (wiping his eyes): Whew! That was one for the books.

Me: I don't want to break it to her, but I'm afraid the hard cheese diet may not be working.

We carried clean dishes hot from the machine to the racks where the plates are kept, then I headed over to fill more baskets with breadsticks. After that, I wasn't nervous anymore. I fell into a good rhythm with Andy and Trish and the time flew by. A strange feeling came over me. I'd never had so much contact with so much food in my life: huge plates of carb-laden pasta covered in cream and butter; bread dripping with fat. Instead of looking good to me, it grossed me out. I kept having to turn my head or race off to find more dishes to carry every time I saw someone shovel a huge bite into their mouths or watched a customer dab a napkin at the butter dripping off his chin.

As I think about it now, there was something amazing and powerful about being around all that food and not being tempted to put a single thing in my mouth. Those people at Parmesan's couldn't control themselves. They were all stuffing their faces, their stomach rolls spilling over the arms of the chairs they'd wedged themselves into. Not me. I was in charge of my body. While everyone else was packing on the weight at the tables all around me, I was speed walking circles around them, getting even thinner than I already am.

As the lunch crowd waddled back to their offices nearby, things died down and the chef served a staff meal. I didn't have a bite. I sat next to Trish after we finished our side work. While she and the other employees ate spaghetti and meatballs I had two glasses of ice water and the two rice cakes I'd brought from home in my purse. As I was clocking out at the computer Melanie came by with my tip out from the waitstaff and told me Andy said I was the best food runner he'd ever worked with. She said it was *highly unusual* but she was going to schedule me for lunch the next day—today—not a training shift, but an actual shift on the floor.

I just got home, and I'm tired, but I feel energized. I did a great job again today, and it sure beats sitting here all day with Mom while Jill is in dance class. Jill texted me on the way home and said she was leaving ballet intensives and that she'd come by later. When I got home, Mom was on her way out the door to work.

Mom: Whew! Sweetheart, you smell good enough to eat.

Me: It's so gross, Mom. The garlic gets on everything.

Mom: There's leftover ham in the fridge and I made a bean casserole.

Me: They made us a staff meal at work.

Mom: Oh, good! I'm glad they feed you during your shift. You need to keep your energy up. I'm so proud of you for getting this job, honey!

She kissed me good-bye and wrapped her arms around me in a big hug. She took a deep breath and sighed.

Mom: Mmmmm. Breadsticks!

Me (laughing): Get out of here.

For a minute after she left, I felt sort of guilty about lying to her. Technically it was just a tiny white lie—not even a lie really. They *had* made us a meal at work. I just didn't eat it. I stood under a hot shower for a long time and washed my hair to get the smell of breadsticks out of it. Once I couldn't smell garlic anymore, I turned off the water and got dressed. I'm almost down to 120 pounds, and all of my shorts are loose. Jill is on her way over right now. She texted me and wants to go shop for jeans. We've both gone down a couple of sizes since we started tracking our calories, and there are back-to-school sales going on now, even though it's the middle of July. Can you believe it? Why is retail in such a hurry to get us back to school? It's like putting up Christmas decorations in October.

Thursday, July 19
Weight: 121

Vanessa and I went running this morning. Geoff has been working with his dad roofing a house early in the mornings before it gets too hot to be up there. I guess I was sort of quiet because Vanessa finally stopped in midsentence and asked if I'd even heard a word she'd said.

The truth is I really hadn't. I was too busy thinking about what happened last night after we got back to Jill's. Jill and I went shopping and both of us got new jeans and a couple of new tops. When we got back to Jill's bedroom, we took everything out and cut the tags off and tried them on in different combinations. Jill calls this Fashion Research. We always have to give outfits a test run together before we wear them out publicly to make sure they pass. Jill pulled on her second new pair of jeans, and the way the fabric hugged her legs was amazing.

Me: I've decided all clothes must be tried on by you first.

Jill (narrowing eyes, staring into mirror): That is ridiculous.

Me: No, what's ridiculous is how great you look in those jeans.

Jill (turning to check the back): They look okay.

Me: Okay?! They look incredible! You could stop traffic on the highway in those jeans.

Jill: They look pretty good, but *good* is often the enemy of the *best*.

Jill peeled off the indigo denim and tossed the pair onto her bed. She slipped the halter top she'd been wearing off over her head and walked over to her desk and pulled a red Magic Marker out of a pencil holder on her desk. It had the word "washable" printed across the side in big bubbly letters, and she handed it to me, then walked over to the tall mirror that leans against the wall next to her closet. It has a dark brown wood frame that goes with Susan's tasteful decorating scheme for the entire house. She stood in front of the mirror in her underwear. The indirect light from the pin spots in her ceiling and the halogen lamp on her desk softly bounced off her skin, accenting every muscle. Years of ballet have given Jill the core strength of a boa constrictor, and the graceful contours of her muscles taut beneath her skin gave her the look of a girl in an advertisement. I just stared at her for a second while she assessed her own body in the mirror. Finally she turned to face me.

Me (holding up marker): What's this?

Jill: There's always room for improvement.

Me: I'm sorry. Are you talking about improving your body?

Jill: Indeed.

Me: I think the only thing on your body that needs improvement is apparently your eyesight.

I moved to where she was standing and turned her shoulders back toward the mirror.

Me: My God, Jill. Your body is perfect.

Jill: No, it's not, but you're going to help me get closer.

Me: How?

Jill: Circle this.

Jill held up her right arm and pointed at the underside of her biceps.

Me: Why?

Jill: There's fat here under my arm.

Me: Where?

Jill: Can't you see that? It's right there. Circle it.

Something about her tone of voice stopped my questions. I took the cap off the marker and drew a red oval around the bottom of her arm as she indicated with her finger. Next, she pointed to the skin below her belly button, tracing with her index finger the path I should draw the circle. She didn't speak for the next few minutes, just pointed and turned, and pointed

142

and turned. It felt like a solemn ceremony of some kind, and as I drew one last circle around her upper thigh, just below the leg opening of her underwear, she began to nod, slowly, then stepped back from the mirror and held out her arms, turning around to survey my bizarre geometry.

Something about this motion—her head nodding, the slow turning, the determined glint in her eyes—was methodical and strange. It sent a chill down my spine, and I stared into the mirror with her, trying to see what Jill must be seeing.

But I couldn't.

It just looked like a bunch of red circles and ovals all over her arms and legs and sides and stomach. There was even one under her chin.

Jill: See? I still have a lot of work to do.

Me: I don't understand.

Wordlessly, Jill turned and smiled at me. It was almost a look of pity. She handed me her phone and told me to snap a picture of her so she could chart her progress. She held her head back so you could see the red circle under her chin but couldn't see her face or tell who she was. Then she took the phone and the red marker out of my hands and walked to her desk, where she opened her laptop and clicked to a website. After tapping and swiping at the screen on her phone several times, she clicked around on the laptop for a second, then brought the computer to her bed and pulled me down next to her.

There was a message forum on the screen, and as Jill scrolled down the page, I saw images of models in ads I recognized from magazines. These pictures had been posted along with candid shots of dancers onstage and girls walking runways, and interspersed between all of these were inspirational quotations like "Craving is only a feeling" and "You've got to fight for every dream." Superimposed over pictures of Kate Moss with her rib cage clearly visible, these sentences seemed to take on a whole new meaning.

Jill clicked to make a new post. She uploaded the picture I'd just taken of her. Underneath the picture she wrote: "Everything that breaks you makes you stronger."

She clicked "submit," and after a few seconds, the picture appeared on the forum under her username: TinyDancer. A few minutes later, comments began to appear:

SkinnyNBones: Wow! Way to go TinyDancer! You have worked so hard.

ThinkThin: #youaremyhero

Thinspiring: Your dedication is uh-MA-zing.

I watched Jill type a response back and add one more picture that was saved on her desktop. It was a picture of a girl lying on her side. She was wearing only a pair of jeans, and you could see her ribs and every vertebra in her back very clearly through her thin skin. Just above her wrist on the inside of her arm there was a tattoo in dark, curly Latin script: "Quod me nutrit, me destruit." Jill typed the translation of the tattoo underneath the image and clicked to post it:

All that nourishes me destroys me.

Jill closed her laptop after that and picked up the red marker.

Jill: Now let's do you.

Me: Let's do *what* to me?

Jill: Circle your goal spots.

Me: No thank you.

Jill (smiling): Oh, c'mon! You helped me. Let me help you.

I shook my head and started gathering my stuff.

Jill: You're not *leaving*, are you?

Me: Yeah, I need to get home. I have to . . .

Jill: You have to what?

The way she leveled her eyes at me made me wince. She knew I was making an excuse. She knew my mom was at work all night. She knew there was nothing waiting for me at home but a big empty house and TV in the dark. Why did this feel so awkward?

Jill: Don't be scared. Be beautiful.

She held out the marker, and we both stood there staring

at it for a moment. Then I smiled at her and picked up the shopping bags with my new jeans inside.

Me: I don't think I'm ready to be quite that . . . beautiful.

Jill smiled as I turned toward her bedroom door, and as I stepped into the hall, I heard her say a single word:

Yet.

I ran into Jack in the kitchen. He and Rob were just coming in from soccer practice and groaning to Susan about having to start two-a-days in a couple weeks.

Jack: Hey, beautiful.

Rob groaned. Susan smiled. I blushed, caught off guard.

Me: Hey, sweaty.

Jack: I clean up real nice.

Me (laughing): So I've heard.

Rob groaned again.

Susan: You're staying for dinner?

Me: No—I have to get home.

She nodded and pecked me on the top of the head as she carried a colander of wet greens from the sink to the cutting board.

Susan: Join us tomorrow? Before you and Jack go . . .

She paused.

Jack: Mini-golf, baaa-by. Gonna tear up some putt-putt.

Rob groaned for a third time, this time loudly. I laughed and said that was my cue to leave, but Jack beat me to the door, spun me around, and kissed me lightly on the lips.

Jack: See you tomorrow.

Me: If you're lucky.

Jack: I always am.

Friday, July 20
Weight: 121

I couldn't get that picture of the girl with the tattoo and her bones poking through her skin out of my head last night. When I woke up this morning it was still there so I went for a run, but it didn't help. I just got out of the shower, and I can still see her.

I just pulled up that website on my tablet. I found Jill's picture with red circles. She's really thin. If she lost any more weight in all of those places she circled, she'd look like the girl with the tattoo. I have a weird feeling in my stomach about that. Somewhere there should be a balance, right? Not a scale, but a *balance* between not being overweight and not being underweight. I think that's what Coach Perkins was trying to do with these food diaries. I weighed myself when I got out of the shower, and I'm down to 121 pounds. I've lost twelve pounds in two months. I'm more in shape than I've ever been. I don't think I need to lose any more.

While I was running this morning, a plan started to form in my mind. I'm going to do a few things.

1. Stop limiting myself to 1,200 calories per day. Coach says I should be eating closer to 2,000, especially if I'm running every day.
2. After practice today, no more lying on my CalorTrack calories. I'm going to honestly type in what I have to eat.
3. I'm going to eat the staff meal at work today. At least I'm going to have a few bites.
4. I'm going to call Dad. I miss him.

Later . . .

Turns out, I didn't have to call Dad. He showed up at lunch today.

I wasn't really paying attention, and when Andy told me we'd just sat at table fourteen, I grabbed two glasses of ice water and a basket of breadsticks and was setting them down on the table before I realized who was sitting in the booth. I get into a zone at work, just running the food, looking for empty plates and half-full water glasses. I don't even look at the faces of the customers that much anymore. Usually they're chunky and chewing with their mouths open. It grosses me out. I might have dropped off the water and breadsticks and left without even noticing but Dad said my name.

Dad: What are you doing here?

Me: I work here. What are you doing here?

Dad: Having lunch. This is Annette.

Dad nodded across the table to a woman with the brightest red hair I'd ever seen and mesmerizing green eyes. She wore a silky white top that swooped low under her emerald blazer. She smiled and said hi. For the first time all day, my Parmesan's Team Smile faded. I couldn't smile, I couldn't say hello back, I couldn't look away. I just stood there holding a basket of breadsticks, staring at this woman.

Have you ever had a moment where you just *know* something out of the blue, no questions asked? I had one of those moments standing in the middle of Parmesan's, my nose full of garlic and ears full of forks scraping the final bits of bottomless salad drenched in Italian dressing from chilled ceramic bowls.

This woman was why Dad left Mom.

I'm sure I only stood there staring for a couple of seconds, but it felt like time stood still. Dad doesn't get flustered easily, but I could tell he was flustered when he spoke again.

Dad: When did you start working here?

Me: When did you stop having Korean barbecue for lunch?

I turned and headed toward the kitchen, blindly. As I walked around the food prep bar toward the dish room I heard Melanie chirp, "Full hands in!" at me, but I didn't stop. I walked past the dishwashers, through the door to dry storage in the corner, and leaned against a big metal rack stacked high with the boxed wine they use in the marinara sauce and to sauté mushrooms. I closed my eyes and took about ten long, deep breaths. All I could see was Annette's face, her bright red lipstick, her bright red hair, her bright green eyes. She was gorgeous.

And thin.

Mom never stood a chance.

I got a quick drink of water and found Melanie at the hot food counter. She took one look at me and knew something was up. I tried to plaster on my Parmesan's smile, but she doesn't miss much.

Melanie: Everything okay?

Me: Fine.

Melanie: Really?

Me: Yep. My dad's here.

Melanie (grinning): Oh, great! Which table?

Andy: Fourteen, and they need more water.

Me: Already?

Andy: Is that thirsty redhead your *mom*?

Me: Are you brain dead?

Melanie thought this was hilarious. I grabbed a pitcher of ice water and Andy followed me with their bowl of salad sputtering apologies. Melanie bought them dessert. Annette didn't eat a single bite. I stood there watching her refuse the bites of cheesecake Dad offered her while he tried to convince me to come to dinner with him the next night. I told him I'd think about it and that I had to go do my side work. He stood up and hugged me. When I tried to step back, he held on for a little bit longer, and something in his touch told me how much he missed me. His cologne smelled like pepper and peach blossoms and I heard myself whispering into his shoulder.

Me: Yes.

Dad: Yes what?

Me: I'll come to dinner.

Dad: Pick you up at seven o'clock.

Me: I'll meet you at Buster's. Some guy bought me this great SUV. I drive it everywhere.

I didn't tell Annette good-bye. I just walked to the back and joined Andy at the staff meal. I drank a glass of water and took a plate of chicken Parmesan. I picked off all the cheese and breading and just ate the chicken. Even without the fat and carbs it was delicious. I had a second piece and a small bowl of salad greens with no dressing. Andy asked me a bunch of questions about Mom and Dad. I answered some of them, then told him I had to go.

Andy: Hot date tonight?

Me: Actually . . . yes.

My head was swimming. Maybe it was all the protein and roughage at once. Or maybe I was overwhelmed from seeing Dad with this Annette chick. Or maybe I just missed Jack.

When I got back home, Mom told me Dad had called her and said he'd seen me and that I'd agreed to go to dinner with him.

Mom: He was at Parmesan's?

Me: Yes. He came in for lunch.

Mom: By himself?

I opened my mouth to lie, but nothing came out. Mom saw in an instant, just like Melanie had earlier. A smile wasn't going to help any of this. And why should I be the one helping? This wasn't my fault.

As I trudged up the stairs to take a shower I heard the cabinets banging and the potato chip bags rustling and the spoon for some ice cream clank on the counter. I wanted to scream down the stairs. I wanted to yell at Mom: WHY DO YOU THINK HE LEFT? But what could I say? I was the one who had gobbled up a cubic ton of chicken during the staff meal. I had decided last night to eat lunch at work today. I told myself it was because I was freaked out by those pictures Jill showed me. Was it really? Maybe I was just eating my feelings too.

I stood in the shower and let the hot water pound onto my head. When I got out the house was still and I knew Mom had left for work. I let out a long, slow sigh and slipped into a clean T-shirt, then slid between the crisp, cool sheets on my bed.

I woke up a few minutes ago. My pillow is damp from falling asleep with wet hair. I'm going to blow it out as soon as I'm done writing. Jack is coming by to pick me up in an hour. I want to look perfect. I need to look perfect. I need to be close to him tonight. I need to feel his arms around me, and taste his lips on mine, and hear him tell me how beautiful I am.

Saturday, July 21
Weight: 120

Jack told me all of that and more.

Mini-golf devolved into Rob making chip shots at the windmill and purposely trying to hit the rotating blades. He finally succeeded, sending an orange golf ball ricocheting directly into Jill's leg. She was furious, and insisted we leave immediately so she could ice the purple welt halfway up her thigh. When we pulled into the driveway at their place, Jill stormed into the house, and Rob moaned and banged his head against the back of Jack's seat three times.

Rob: Why do I *do* this shit?

Jack (smirking): You're a glutton for punishment.

Rob: Or maybe I just like the makeup make-out session.

Jack (not smirking): Don't. Make. Me. Come. Back. There.

Rob got out of the car quickly. Jack rolled his eyes.

Jack: It's a good thing I like him. He's a scoundrel.

Me: I'm pretty sure Jill doesn't let him get away with a thing.

Jack: The question is, are *you* going to let me get away with anything?

Me (Southern accent): Why I de-*clare*, Mister Jack.

Jack laughed and reached over to take my hand. He brought it to his lips and kissed my fingers. He held on to it while he backed out of the driveway again, and as the moon rose over the mountain, we drove in silence. It was a comfortable silence, not a loaded one—no pregnant pause. It wasn't that either of us had something to say and was holding it back. Everything that needed to be expressed was happening in the way he laced his fingers through mine, and the way my thumb kept time with the music on the back of his hand.

I finally understood the phrase "Less is more."

Jack pulled into an industrial park behind the little airport in the center of town. He drove between the low adobe buildings filled with stores that sell construction contractors their windows, doors, and fixtures, scuba divers their gear, and mechanics their auto parts. Behind the last row of self-storage units was a twelve-foot-high chain-link fence that ran along the runway. Jack backed up against the fence, then pulled a stadium blanket out of his extended cab behind the seat. As the moon rose higher in the sky, we lay on our backs in the bed of his truck, holding hands, listening to the roar of the plane engines drown out the sound of the music filtering through the open window at the back of the cab.

Eventually, Jack rolled over on one elbow and stared at me. I felt his eyes on my face, then his hand sliding across my stomach, tucking beneath me, pulling me close to him. Both of his hands gripped my waist, and I realized that his fingers almost touched on either side. Something about this made me smile, and he smiled back.

Jack: You have such an amazing body. It's perfect.

I didn't speak, but I let my lips do the talking. I felt him pressing into me with that same reckless abandon he'd had on the deck of the boat last month, and I knew it was because he wanted me. I felt the thrill of his touch and the strength in his arms and legs. I recognized the fierce nature I'd stirred up inside him, and relished his passion. He wanted my body—this new, beautiful body of mine—and as his hands explored every inch of me, this time they slid under my clothes, taking my breath with their warmth and their tenderness. His hands were everywhere, his touch making me sure of his feelings for me even before he whispered, "I love you," into my ear. When he did, something rushed through me like the roar of the jets overhead, and using my perfect body, I assured him I felt the same without ever saying a word.

Saturday, July 21
Weight: 120.5

I can't believe he brought her.

When I walked into Buster's, Annette was sitting there next to him in the booth, smiling like it was Christmas morning and Santa had brought her a pony. When I saw her, I stopped short and just stared. When Dad spotted me and waved, he nudged her to slide over so he could get out of the booth, and she actually jumped up grinning, ran up to me, and gave me a hug.

A hug.

She pressed her enormous boobs, which were spilling out of her little strappy tank top, against me and said that it was great to see me again. Then Dad took a turn hugging me, and I whispered in his ear.

Me: Um . . . what is *she* doing here?

He tried to pull away, but I kept my arms around him, so his ear was close to my shoulder as he stuttered.

Dad: I . . . I . . . just . . . thought . . .

I plastered on my Parmesan's smile and peered over his shoulder at Annette.

Me: Would you excuse us just for a second? My mom gave me some stuff to give Dad, and I want to make sure I don't forget to get it out of the car later.

Annette nodded enthusiastically, and Dad sputtered protests as I dragged him by the hand into the parking lot, my smile now a grim line of determination drawn across my face, my cheeks hot with anger. In the parking lot, I let him have it.

Me: What the *hell* are you doing?

Dad: Now wait just a second—

Me: Nope. You don't get to talk right now. You get to listen. I did not sign up to have dinner with you and whoever that is, tonight. I agreed to have dinner with *you*.

His face clouded, and he crossed his arms like a toddler.

Dad: Her name is *Annette*. She's the office manager at the dealership. And she's my girlfriend.

Me: Really, Dad? *Really?* It's been what? Two months? Not even. It's been like *six weeks* since you walked out on me and Mom, and I'm just supposed to show up and have dinner with you and the chick with the tits in there?

Dad: You watch your mouth, young lady.

Me: I'll watch it all the way to my car.

I didn't look back as I walked to the enormous car he bought me. I didn't want him to see the tears sliding down my cheeks. He doesn't deserve to see me cry.

I get it that Mom is not a skinny, big-chested model. I understand that's what he wanted. I'd rather look like her than Mom, too. But he's my *dad*. Isn't he supposed to care about my feelings a little bit? Shouldn't he want to talk things over with me one-on-one at least *once* before I'm required to start having "family meals" with Boobalicious the office manager?

The worst part of it was that he didn't try to stop me. He didn't try to follow me. He just stood there in the parking lot and watched me go. This was supposed to be a special night. It was supposed to be this time when we regrouped, and talked, and cried—when he told me how sorry he was and when I told him that I understood more than he thought I did.

This was supposed to be the night when our relationship grew up. When he stopped being just my dad and started being my friend. I don't let my friends treat me this way. I'm not going to let him treat me this way either. I don't care if I never see him again.

It's just as well. There was nothing I could eat at Buster's anyway.

Sunday, July 22
Weight: 120

158

Couldn't sleep last night. Seeing Dad again ripped the scab off, and I couldn't stop thinking about him and Mom and everything that went wrong. Mom was up and in the kitchen in her sweatpants eating Lucky Charms and chirping to Pam on the phone. She was chewing with her mouth open and laughing really loudly, and I just couldn't deal with it. I drank three glasses of water, then brought a cup of coffee and a hard-boiled egg back up here to my room.

All I know for sure is that it grosses me out to watch Mom eat and act like that, and as much as Dad shouldn't have brought Annette to dinner last night, I can't blame him for wanting to be with her. In any sort of side-by-side comparison, Annette wins over Mom every time in the looks department.

As I finished my egg I glanced down at a picture of me and Mom and Dad on my desk. I was four years old, and we were at the water park here in town. I don't know who took this picture. Dad probably asked some stranger. Dad's tan and young and has a goatee. Mom isn't skinny, but she's curvy in all the right places. She's wearing a black one-piece suit that is cut just right for her figure and dark glasses. Her smile is beautiful and relaxed. She's laughing along with me as we try to pose in the shallow end of the wave pool.

We look happy.

I can't help but think we'd still be happy if Mom still looked like she does in this photo.

I was thinking about this and sipping my coffee as I opened my laptop. Maybe it was the caffeine, or maybe it was the web address I was typing into the browser, but my heart started to race as I scrolled the pictures on the site Jill showed me on Thursday. These girls are thin like Jill is. I remembered how Jack's hands had fit around my waist as he pulled me against him in the back of his truck. These girls in the pictures know what that feels like. They have control of their lives like Susan and Jill. They are the opposite of my mother.

I will be like them. I will have more willpower than my mother. I will not let Jack leave me the way Mom let Dad leave her.

Sunday, August 26
Weight: 119

School starts tomorrow. Jill just left. We planned our outfits and she posted the following on the website:

THE THIN COMMANDMENTS

1. Thin = Attractive. If you are not thin, you are not attractive.

2. Thou shalt do everything within your power to make yourself look thinner. This includes clothing, hairstyle, exercise, and taking laxatives when needed.

3. Thou shalt not eat without feeling guilty.

4. Thou shalt punish yourself for eating fattening foods.

5. Thou shalt always count and restrict your calories.

6. Thou shalt remember that what the scale says is the most important thing.

7. Being thin is more important than being healthy.

8. There is no such thing as "too thin."

9. Restricting calories and staying thin are the measure of true willpower and success.

I printed out a copy and taped it inside my notebook. I took a picture of it with my phone, so I can look at it if I'm feeling tempted.

Jill is down to only a hundred pounds. All of those areas she circled last month have somehow gotten smaller. I stopped writing for a while because all I could think about was Dad, and I didn't want to deal with it. I've been running every day whether Vanessa comes or not. I've kept my calories down to around 1,200 to 1,500 per day. Jill is restricting hers to 1,000 to 1,200 per day. She's never danced better. I've never had better times running.

I don't care if Vanessa is "concerned."

I'm fine.

I'm better than fine.

I'm better than ever.

(Just ask Jack.)

Sunday, September 2

Weight: 119

I came in second place at the invitational yesterday. Our team won the meet for the first time in four years. Coach Perkins hugged me and jumped up and down and cried when I crossed the finish line. Afterward, she gathered everybody and announced her decision to make me team captain. She told everyone that I was an example of what you could do if you put your mind to it and trained like a champion. Vanessa and Geoff could barely look at me, but I didn't care.

We won.

I won.

Dad showed up at the meet. No Annette. He gave me a hug

and told me he was proud of me. He should be. I kicked butt. He wanted to take me out to dinner, but I saw Mom standing at the edge of the parking lot talking to Jack and Rob, and I told Dad I had to go. Jack asked Mom if she wanted to come with us to get dinner after the race. She had to run home and then head to work, but it was just like Jack to offer.

We went to meet Rob and Jill at this restaurant where they bake your pizza in a wood-fire oven. Rob and Jack ate an entire pig's worth of pepperoni. I had a salad with Jill, dressing on the side, and I decided to allow myself a single glorious slice. I chewed the first bite slowly, and the gooey, salty, greasy deliciousness ran across my tongue and made my eyes roll back in my head. It was the best pizza I'd ever tasted. Then I took a second bite, and I realized something:

It never tastes any better than the first bite.

I put the slice back down on the plate while Rob and Jack ordered more Coke and talked to a guy from the soccer team they ran into, and Jill was checking a voice mail message on her phone. I thought about the salad I'd eaten most of, except for the croutons, and the bit of pizza I'd just swallowed, and I realized I was full. I didn't need the rest of that piece of pizza. I'd already enjoyed the first bite, and it was never going to taste any better than that.

The thought was like a cool breeze on a warm day, and I smiled really big at Jack as he and Rob finished talking to their friend and came back to the table. Just as they sat down, Jill's eyes went wide with the phone pressed to her ear and she started squealing and laughing and hopping up and down in the booth, and then tears started streaming down her cheeks.

Jill: I got it! I got it!

Rob: Holy cow. Watch it! You're gonna spill your water!

Me: Are you okay?

Jill: I'm better than okay. I'm *Clara* in the mother-effing *Nutcracker*!

Jack and I cheered like idiots, and we dragged her out of the booth and hugged her in the middle of the restaurant. I'm sure everybody thought we'd lost our minds. I didn't care. This is what discipline looks like. This is what willpower looks like.

Take *that*, Misty Jenkins.

Saturday, September 8
Weight: 119

Jack asked me to homecoming.

That sentence is amazing all by itself, but what's even more incredible is the *way* he asked me to homecoming. I went to Jill's last night after practice. Mom was already at work, so we hung out with James and Susan, who were watching some old romantic comedy about a hockey player and a figure skater who fall in love. Jill crushed up four rice cakes in a big bowl and made us "skinny-girl popcorn." If you pour enough salt on them, it almost works. I kept expecting Jack to come home, but James told me he and Rob were out shopping for supplies for some sort of science project they had to put together.

Rob and Jack arrived as the credits were rolling and both of them squeezed in next to us on the giant chesterfield sofa. Jack grinned and kissed me on the cheek. We talked with his parents for a while, then he asked if I wanted to go get yogurt at YouGoYum. I looked at Jill with raised eyebrows and she held up a hand like a stop sign.

Jill: No carbs for Clara.

Rob (yawning): Yeah, I gotta get home. My pops wants me to help him paint the garage door in the morning.

Me (to Jack): Shall I drive or do you want to?

Jack: I'll drive.

We held hands all the way there, and when Jack made a large swirl with caramel, hot fudge, bananas, and walnuts, I told him I'd just have a bite of his. The first bite was delicious. The second one he held out I politely declined. He shook his head.

Jack: I don't know how you do it.

Me: Do what?

Jack: Stay so disciplined—and gorgeous. You're like an Olympic athlete or something.

I decided to let him in on my newfound secret, and shrugged.

Me: It never tastes any better than the first bite.

He laughed and shook his head, then wolfed down the rest of his yogurt and dragged me back to the car. When we got to the intersection where he should have gone right to head to his house, he turned left and drove toward mine. Before I registered that my car was still at his place, we were turning into the driveway at mine, and as we did, a huge lit sign across the garage door blinked. There must've been *hundreds* of little white lights that spelled out my name and the words "Will You Go to Homecoming With Me? Love Jack." He had to have spent *hours* working on it—punching holes through giant sheets of foam board and arranging all the letters just right.

I sat there in shock as Jack reached behind the seat and pulled out a dozen roses.

Me: But—how did—

Jack: There's no science project. Well, there is, but Rob and I weren't shopping for that.

Me: How . . . ?

Jack: Did we turn them on? It's a timer. I nabbed a house key from your mom last week at your meet so we could set it up.

There were tears in my eyes. I'd always gone to the dances at school with either a random guy I didn't really like or as Geoff

166

and Vanessa's third wheel. Now, for the first time, I was going to go with a boy that I really cared for—and not just any boy. I was going with Jack, the best-looking one of the popular senior guys.

Jack: Cat got your tongue?

Me: I . . . I can't—

Jack (whispering): Move over, cat. It's my turn.

He kissed me so gently and sweetly and fully on the mouth that the tears in my eyes spilled down my cheeks from the sheer joy of being me, in my skin, in my life at that moment. He kissed my neck and whispered in my ear.

Jack: Every taste of you is better than the last.

Jill was still up waiting for us when we got back to their house. Rob hadn't gone anywhere either. Everybody had been in on it, and we stayed up late in the hot tub, then I texted Mom at work that I was going to sleep over at Jill's, and this morning we went dress shopping for formals with Susan to celebrate.

Susan insisted on buying me a dress.

Susan: Please. Your poor mom is probably too exhausted from working her tail off to join us. I'll get the money from her later. *Besides*, this is a special occasion. We're celebrating what a great job you girls are already doing. Winning cross-country meets and ballet roles. I'm just so *proud* of you. Not to mention, you look *fabulous*.

Jill tried on seventeen dresses before choosing the first one she'd picked up (naturally), a short black sequined sheath with a black tulle pouf that wrapped on one shoulder. I tried on four but kept coming back to a dress I didn't have the nerve to pick up. Susan saw me eyeing it because when I opened the dressing room door, she was standing there holding it.

It was simple red organza silk, not shiny, but rich, textured and bright. It was fitted at the top with a plunging neckline and back line. No beads, no prints, no bangles, no tassels or trim. It just fell to a pool behind my feet with the tiniest train. When I opened the dressing room door so Susan could zip the back, Jill caught a glimpse of the front in the mirror and gasped.

Jill: That's it.

Me: I'm not sure if I can pull this off. It seems a little . . .

Jill: Dramatic. It's *amazing*.

Susan: I can almost get it closed. What size is this?

Me: It's a two. I'm really a four.

Susan: No, you're right in between. Let's get you this. You have six weeks and all you need to do is take off a couple more pounds and it'll be stunning.

Me: Are you sure?

Susan turned me back toward the mirror and told me to stand up straight. I did.

Susan: Now on your toes like you're wearing heels.

When I stood up on my toes, the hem at the front of

the dress cascaded down, just brushing the floor, and at that moment, Susan took my long blond hair from behind and wrapped it skillfully into a makeshift French twist, just like hers.

The effect was startling.

Jill: Wow.

Susan: This is the dress. You look like Grace Kelly.

Me: You really think I can do it?

Jill: As of right now, you don't have a choice.

This afternoon, Jill gave me something she calls "ballerina tea." It's made from the leaves of a plant that helps your body "cleanse." She told me to drink a mug every day, and then again at night before bed, but not to drink it before I was going to leave the house for anything important. I just had my first mug, and about an hour later I had my first "cleanse." She wasn't kidding. I'm going to have to stay close to home drinking this tea.

I'm sitting here staring at this dress hanging on my closet door. I'm feeling a little panicked about being able to fit into it, but I *have* to. I will *never forgive myself* if I don't. Mom came in a few minutes ago and asked me how it all went. I showed her the pictures I took of the sign on the garage door last night, and she hugged me. For just a minute, it was like I forgot all about the problems with her and Dad and how annoyed with her I've been lately. She was so happy for me.

Mom: Jack is a *good guy*.

Me (smiling): Yeah . . . he's pretty special.

Mom: Now! Let me see you in this dress!

It took me a minute to convince her that I needed to shower before I put it on, and that I really needed to find the right shoes first, and she wouldn't leave me alone about it until I promised her that we'd go shop for shoes together tomorrow. She wrote me a check to give to Susan for the dress and told me she was sorry she'd been so out of it and working so much. Now she's back downstairs, and I can hear the TV.

The work begins now. I know what I have to do. I have six weeks to fit in this dress, and I intend to if it's the last thing I do.

First I'm going to run.

Then I need to find a red marker.

Sunday, September 9
Weight: 118.5

I don't understand my mother. You'd think that after all she's been through, she'd see what I'm doing—what I'm trying to do, the sacrifices I'm making—and put it all together. You'd think she'd be able to see that I'm just trying my hardest not to end up unhappy and divorced. Instead, she's bound and determined to make me as miserable as she is.

It happened after my run yesterday morning. Usually, after I run, I feel *better* about things, but for some reason, when I walked into my bedroom and pulled off my sweaty clothes, I saw my homecoming dress hanging on the closet door and I just felt panicked. I caught a glimpse of my body in the mirror, and it looked way too big to *ever* fit into that beautiful red gown, and the idea of not being able to wear that dress in six weeks when Jack comes to pick me up in his tuxedo made me start to cry.

Usually I'm not so emotional, but I'd just run five and a half miles, and all I could see in the mirror yesterday were all the places on my body that stretched against that beautiful red size-two dress.

I dug through my desk until I found a red marker and stood in front of my mirror just like I'd seen Jill do. I circled every part of my stomach and hips and arms and chest that needed to go away, but it just seemed like the red circles on my skin made those places grow and swell until they were like gross, sagging bags of fat swinging from my body. I started to cry harder, and right at that very second, I realized I hadn't locked my door—just as Mom knocked softly and opened it to see if I was all right.

I saw from the look on her face that she knew *exactly* what I was doing. I screamed at her to get out of my room, and she didn't say anything or move at all. She just stood at the door, her mouth open, but no sound coming out.

I threw myself down on the bed and pulled my comforter over me and cried. I lay there for a long time, sobbing into my pillow, until I thought she was probably gone, but then I felt her hand on my back as she sat down next to me on the bed.

I thought she was going to lecture me.

I thought she was going to tell me all the things I already know about what she's afraid will happen to me.

Instead she just helped me up and into the shower, and when I got out there was a note on my pillow that said:

Come find me when you want to talk.

I love you.

Mom

I don't want to talk to her about this right now.

I don't think I can avoid her forever.

Monday, September 10
Weight: 118

Mom was waiting for me in the kitchen just now when I woke up. She was standing there with a big smile on her face and had a bowl of oatmeal with yogurt and strawberries on top. There was one for each of us. She asked me if I wanted coffee, and I told her I was going to make some tea. Thank God Jill gave me this stuff because Mom forced me to choke down the entire bowl of oatmeal. When I put it all into the CalorTrack app just now it was over four hundred calories with the berries and the yogurt.

I didn't try to argue with her. I knew that would just make things worse. Every bite felt like it lodged in my stomach, and I can feel it hanging there inside of me, making all the spots I circled last night stick out, making it impossible for me to fit into that dress.

The food wasn't the worst part of breakfast. No, it was Mom's new rules. She went on and on about the dangers of teenage girls and calorie restriction and the girls she's seen come into the ER who are so underweight that they can't hold a spoon and have permanent heart damage. I hadn't seen Mom this alive and fired up since Dad left. I have unwittingly given her a purpose in life now: keeping me as fat as she can.

So now, not only do I have to lose eight pounds in six weeks, I have to do it in spite of being forced to eat breakfast with Mom every morning before I go to school. This is her new requirement for letting me out the door.

Fine.

I'll just get up earlier and run before school. I'll put myself on two-a-day runs. I'll go in the morning before I have to eat breakfast and in the afternoon at practice. This is who I am now: the girl who doesn't back down. I will fit into that dress in six weeks. Nothing and no one will stop me. Not Mom. Not oatmeal. Not my own lack of discipline.

The tea just kicked in. Gotta run.

Wednesday, September 12
Weight: 118

Part of me is seething inside. Part of me wants to run down the hall right now after my mom and scratch her eyes out. I'm going to write until that part of me is silenced.

That's the part of me that is out of control, the part of me that must be contained. That's the part of me that will cause me to lose it and go berserk, to stuff my face with anything it sees to make these feelings go away.

I just got home from practice and passed Mom in the hall.

Mom: Did you talk to Coach Perkins?

Me: Yeah.

Mom: Everything okay, sweetie?

Me (Parmesan's smile): Yep! Everything's cool.

Mom: Good. I love you so much. I left you a barbecue chicken breast and some mashed potatoes on the counter.

Me: Thanks! I'm going to take a shower. Have a good night at work.

The fact that she called Coach Perkins makes me want to throw things. I closed the door and listened for the garage to open and close behind her. Then I hit my bed with a pillow about twenty times. When Coach asked me to stay behind after practice, I saw Vanessa's eyes shoot over at me, and I just *knew* she was hoping I was going to get into trouble. Coach was pretty calm about the whole thing, just said Mom was "concerned" and she wanted to make sure I was being truthful about my calories.

Coach: You're running better than you ever have. I just want to make sure you can keep it up.

Me: Everything is fine. Mom is just worried because I've lost a few pounds.

Coach: I know you've had a hard summer, but I want to make sure you keep winning. You have to eat right to make that happen.

Me: I'm eating a ton.

Coach: Winning is not more important than your health.

My face was so red it must've looked like it was going to catch fire. Vanessa tried to follow me to my car, but I walked right past her. She and Geoff still eat with us every day at lunch, but I can barely talk to her. She just doesn't understand. She doesn't get it.

Jill just texted me back. I'm going to meet her at the park to do our workout.

Right after I bury those mashed potatoes in the outside trash can.

Thursday, September 13
Weight: 117

My mother is going to destroy me. She announced this morning over yet another bowl of carbohydrate-filled oatmeal sprinkled with fattening, sugary dried fruit pieces that she has decided to transfer to the day shift.

Why?

Well, me of course. She thinks I must be fed like a toddler. After talking with Coach Perkins on the phone about our little chat on Wednesday, she thinks it would be best if we "spent more time together. Especially *dinnertime.*"

I could barely contain my rage.

But I did it.

My lip quivered, and my Parmesan's smile failed me, but I managed a nod and a quick "Great, Mom" and kept from shattering my bowl in the sink until she'd gone upstairs to get in the shower. By the time she was done, I had cleaned up the porcelain shards and was on my way out the door to school.

As I pulled into the parking lot, I took a deep breath, knowing that surely the very worst part of my day was over. I'd been up since 6 a.m., after all. I'd run a fast-paced five-miler, then showered, pooped, and weighed myself to find the scale said I was exactly where I'd been yesterday. Then I'd had to suffer through yet another breakfast while dealing with the worst news ever from Mom. This means she'll be hovering over me in the morning at breakfast, and again at night, when I usually don't have to eat anything after school. Now I'll have to contend with her at dinner at 8 p.m.

I cannot eat that late at night.

But no matter. I was finally at school. Jill brought me more tea bags. They kicked in during second period. We planned and strategized. We would meet and work out every night after my cross-country practice. I'd do double the running and double the workouts. From here, everything would look up. Nothing could make the day any more terrible.

Then Vanessa sat down at lunch. She reached across the table in front of Geoff, Rob, Jack, and Jill and grabbed my hand.

Vanessa (concerned): How did it go with Coach Perkins?

My blood froze.

Rob: How did *what* go with Coach Perkins?

Me: Nothing. It's fine.

Vanessa: Did she ask you about your food diary?

Me (firmly): Everything. Is. Fine.

I don't think I could have shot a more fierce look at her across the table, but it was like Vanessa was operating under a force field.

Vanessa: I just worry about you. You and Jill never eat very much.

Jill (icily): We eat plenty. And it's none of your business.

Vanessa (turning to me): It's just that you're so . . .

Jack: Beautiful?

It wasn't like him to jump in or even really pay attention to Vanessa, but all of a sudden his arm was around me, and I felt the warmth of his body on my shoulders. His gaze silenced Vanessa, and Geoff made some sort of stupid joke. Then Rob jumped in and started talking about the limo the guys want to rent for homecoming.

Jack kept his arm around my shoulders during lunch and walked me down the hall to my locker after we left the cafeteria.

Jack: She's just jealous.

Me: Really, I'm not worried about it.

Jack: She just wishes she was as fast as you, or as gorgeous.

He reached down and lifted my chin and kissed me lightly on the lips right there in the middle of the hall.

I went straight to the park after running and worked out with Jill. Mom still has a week and a half on the night shift, so when I came home, I did the whole workout again in my bedroom. Then I lay on the floor staring at the red dress in the clear plastic wrapper. All I could hear were Vanessa's words in my head. She acts so *concerned*, like it's her very own Lifetime movie and she's the best friend trying to keep everyone from going off the rails.

How dare she bring up my weight or my looks or my eating habits in front of Jack?

I looked around my room at all the little-girl crap that is still everywhere, and I couldn't stand the clutter anymore. I don't want stuffed animals in my bedroom. I don't want cute and cuddly. I don't want anything that reminds me of my dad, or my mom's knickknack crap all over everything. I want things to be clean and organized.

I raced down the stairs and grabbed garbage bags and started filling them up with all the lacy, frilly crap my mom puts everywhere. The flowers she dried for me from the Valentine's bouquet she gave me last year. The silly spoons and bells she used to bring back from all over the country when we went on vacation for "my collection."

This crap was never mine. It was hers.

I hauled most of it out to the trash. I kept a bag of stuffed animals and put them on the shelves in the garage next to a plastic bin of Christmas decorations. Then I vacuumed and dusted and straightened and organized until my room looked like a place where I wanted to be—a place of clean, sharp edges and symmetry, well arranged, with nothing but the absolute essentials, and the red dress, hanging on the closet door, reminding me that I can do anything, that I *must* do anything required to stay on track.

I can feel the places that I circled with that marker pulsing on my skin as I write this. I can feel that all my hard work today has paid off. I hope the scale won't tell a different story tmorrow.

Friday, September 14
Weight: 115.7

I am almost halfway to my goal. When I saw what the scale said this morning, I knew I was doing the right things. At school, Jill agreed, and hugged me when I told her how I was only five pounds away from 110. She texted me a link to a page of negative-calorie foods during second period. Negative calorie supposedly means that it actually burns more calories to digest the food than the food contains. The result is that your stomach is full, but your body burns up the calories from the food as you digest it.

Today at lunch, Vanessa and Geoff were right behind me in the lunch line at the salad bar in the cafeteria. My plate was piled high with the foods on the list Jill sent me: apple slices, celery sticks, and raw spinach.

Vanessa: Um . . . how are you going to make your calorie requirement for Coach if you're only eating apple slices and celery sticks? Don't you want some protein?

I pulled a bag of gummy fruit snacks out of my purse and tossed them onto the tray. I hadn't put one in my mouth for at least a couple of months, but she didn't need to know that. I like having them in my purse because it reminds me that I'm the one in control. At any moment, I could reach in and pour pure corn syrup down my throat.

But I don't.

Vanessa looked at the fruit snacks, then up at me. I could see the suspicion in her eyes.

Me: See? I eat. Lay off.

She opened her mouth again to speak. Geoff nudged her and shook his head.

Maybe Geoff is smarter than he lets on.

Tuesday, September 25
Weight: 114.5

I hate myself for begging. That was the worst part of it. I never want to be reduced to that again.

Vanessa was waiting for me at my locker today before we went to practice. I was grabbing the printout of my calories from the CalorTrack app when my ring slipped off my finger. It's from Tiffany. Mom gave it to me for my fifteenth birthday last year, and I tossed my books into my locker and hit my hands and knees. Everybody around me in the hall kept walking and tripping over me, and I saw the ring get kicked twice before I finally nabbed it.

I didn't understand why Vanessa wasn't helping me direct traffic or find the ring, until I stood up and saw her face. Apparently, all of my books had tumbled back out of the locker and she had scooped them up. When she did, she saw this notebook—the original food diary.

Her face was pale. She looked like she was going to cry. She held it out to me as I walked back toward her at the locker, a sinking feeling in my stomach that turned to panic.

Me: Wait. Vanessa. Wait.

Vanessa: What is *this*? What are you *doing*?

Me: Vanessa, it's not that big a deal. It's not—

Vanessa: It *is* a big deal. It is a *very* big deal. You are going to tell Coach right now, or I will.

That's when I started begging.

And bargaining.

And promising her anything.

She finally said she wouldn't tell Coach on one condition: That I start eating again. Every meal. Every bite. Enough calories. The recommended amount of 2,200 per day for my height and activity level.

She made me promise.

She made me swear.

I've still got four pounds to lose before two weeks from Saturday. I don't care what I said to Vanessa. I'm going to make it happen.

Wednesday, September 26

Weight: 114

Today is Mom's first day shift. She looked a little frazzled and I think it's going to take her some time to get on a normal sleep schedule. She just buzzed around the kitchen dropping things, and it took her three tries to get to the car after breakfast. She kept having to come in and get stuff: keys, sunglasses, wallet.

Something I realized as I sat there eating my required breakfast in front of her: she wasn't really watching me. I took a bite and then swallowed it, then took another bite and spit it out in my napkin when she wasn't looking. She didn't even notice. After that, I realized I could throw most of my oatmeal away in my paper napkin.

When the bowl was empty, I took it to the sink and rinsed it out. She kissed me on the cheek and scooted out to the garage for the third time. I made another mug of ballerina tea to keep the bites I did swallow moving on through me.

I have no idea what to expect tonight.

Later . . .

Dinner.

That's what I had to expect.

And of course, she made a big deal of it. She insisted we go out to get burgers at Buster's. I got a protein-style, and I didn't get any fries or onion rings.

Mom chirped on and on about how great it was going to be to finally work days like a normal person and not feel like a vampire. She's *very excited* about getting to spend more time with me, and talked about all the special dinners we could have together. She *totally understands* that I want to eat healthily so she talked and talked and talked about the food she was going to make me.

I'd never been so happy to see my phone light up when Dad called in the middle of her lemon-pepper chicken recipe. I pointed at my phone and said, "Dad," which stopped her midsentence, then I took a huge bite of hamburger and held it in my mouth as I slipped out of the booth and answered the

184

phone with the wad of ground beef on one side of my mouth.

Dad: Hey, honey! Glad I got you on the phone.

Me: Hi.

Dad: Are you . . . eating? Did I call at a bad time?

Me: Hang on.

I pushed through the bathroom door and spit the huge bite of burger into the trash can. It was quieter in here.

Me: Hi. Sorry. Mom and I are at Buster's.

Dad: Oh! Great. Listen, I was wondering if you wanted to come over and stay the weekend at my place. Or maybe even Friday night? We could go to your meet together on Saturday? I finally got the guest room all set up and . . .

His voice trailed off. I just stood there waiting. It felt like I was supposed to say something now, and I didn't know what. I hated these silences between us now. Like it was somehow my job to be perky and cheerful and make everyone feel better about the crap they were putting me through.

Dad: You there?

Me: Yeah. Um . . . maybe . . . some other weekend, Dad. It's just . . . this weekend is really busy. I know you work late on Friday, and the meet is early on Saturday, and I have a date that night.

Dad: A date, huh?

Me: Yeah. Dad, I have to go.

Dad: Okay, sweetheart. Well, maybe the next weekend?

Me: Sure. Maybe, I'll look at my calendar.

He told me he loved me and then he hung up. All of a sudden, my stomach cramped up. I raced into a stall and threw up the bites of the burger I'd eaten.

Turns out there's a silver lining to phone calls from Dad after all.

Sunday, September 30
Weight: 113

I just got home from the hospital.

I sat and stared at that first sentence for a little while after I wrote it. I still can't believe I collapsed during the meet yesterday.

I didn't feel bad yesterday morning. The gun went off, and we started running. I pulled away from the pack with Vanessa right behind me, and two girls from the Riverside team in front of me. I don't like to try to run in the lead because it makes me nervous. I'm always looking over my shoulder for someone to be nipping at my heels. I like to hang back until I can tell the leaders are getting winded, then I try to make a move and come from behind in the last mile. The trick is not getting too far behind.

After two miles through the wash along the back edge
of the school, we doubled back, following the markers along
a golf course, and the mountains came into full view. They
were majestic in shades of purple and blue, summits of torn
construction paper stretched across the sky. Their fuzzy,
jagged edges reached up toward the bright rays of the sun,
which warmed my face. Everything else seemed to fall away. I
stretched out my stride and made my move on the Riverside
girls, sailing past them in a burst of speed. Now it was only me,
out in front with a mile to go, then a half mile, then a quarter
mile. I rounded the back of the fine arts building into the
roped-off course that led toward the track. I heard the cheers
of the small crowd of parents and friends watching from the
bleachers near the finish line. I felt a rush through my head like
a buzzing, and a smile formed on my lips. I sped up as I raced
across the grass toward the edge of the track. I could hear my
own heartbeat pounding in my ears as the white-hot light of the
sun filled my eyes and then . . .

I heard a beep.

BEEP

BEEP

BEEP

BEEP

. . . and a voice:

Do you know where you are?

Can you tell me your name?

Do you know what day it is?

Slowly, the bright, white light of the sun narrowed into a single beam, which came from the end of a tiny penlight held by a woman with dark skin in a white jacket. She was asking me the questions.

Do you know where you are?

Do you know what happened?

Can you hear me?

I answered her questions:

No.

No.

Yes.

I looked around and slowly other faces came into focus: Mom, her mascara running down her cheeks; Dad, his eyes red and frightened; Coach Perkins, her lips set in a thin, straight line.

The woman in the white jacket was Dr. Nash, a friend of Mom's from the hospital, which is where I was.

Mom said I'd collapsed during the race.

Dr. Nash said I was dehydrated and beginning to show signs of malnourishment.

Coach Perkins said she'd gone over my CalorTrack printouts

and she had some questions about what I'd been eating.

Dad couldn't say anything. He just stared at me, lying there in the bed with a tube pumping fluids into my arm.

Mom said I had to start eating more.

Dr. Nash said I had to stay overnight for observation.

Coach said I was benched until I gained some weight.

Dad ran his hand over his face, kissed my forehead, and walked into the hallway, and I fell back asleep for what felt like a very long time.

When I opened my eyes this morning at 6:12 a.m., Mom was sleeping in the chair next to my bed. I guess she'd been there all night long. She had a blanket wrapped around her, and it was just the two of us, the beep of my heart monitor, and the gentle sound of her breathing, in and out, peaceful and slow.

My head felt clear, and I wasn't tired. There was a vase with bright yellow gerbera daisies and purple statice sitting on the little table next to the bed. I lay there trying to remember if they'd been there yesterday. I couldn't. I tried to remember anything at all between racing for the finish line and winding up in a hospital bed, but I couldn't. I watched Mom sleep in the chair, and I wondered where Dad had gone when he left.

Mom woke up when a couple of nurses who she works with in the ER came to check on us. When they went back downstairs, Mom told me Jack had come by yesterday evening, but I was sound asleep. He wouldn't let her wake me; he just left the flowers. When I checked my phone there was a single text from him:

Hope you're feeling better. I love you.

After I read that, I did feel better, even when Mom and Dr. Nash insisted I eat two bowls of Jell-O and a plate of scrambled eggs with cheese in front of them. As I ate, they asked me questions:

Had I been limiting my calories instead of keeping the goal set by Coach?

Why did I feel I needed to lose weight?

Did I know how dangerous it was for my heart and kidneys to be running long distances without proper nutrition?

Did I understand the long-term effects of not eating enough calories?

I answered all the questions correctly, but all I could hear in my head as I swallowed the cool, sweet gelatin squares was Susan's voice in my head:

Carbs are killing us.

Before she left the room, Dr. Nash looked right into my eyes and put a hand on my shoulder.

Dr. Nash: You are dangerously thin. You're a pretty girl, but you are more than ten pounds underweight. A young woman who is five seven should weigh well over 120 pounds; with your athletic frame, closer to 130. When was the last time you had your period?

I didn't say anything.

Mom: Sweetheart?

Dr. Nash: Did you have it this month?

I couldn't look at her. I shook my head.

Dr. Nash: Last month.

Me: No.

She turned to my mom.

Dr. Nash: We have worked together for how many years now?

Mom: Almost ten . . .

Dr. Nash: Would I lie to you?

Mom: No.

Dr. Nash: I need both of y'all to hear this. If you don't start eating more calories every day, you will be back. And if you come back, I'm going to send you to the thirteenth floor.

Mom has talked about the thirteenth floor for years. It's the psych ward, the floor in the hospital with a series of locked doors between the patients and the elevators.

Mom was quiet on the way home. When we walked into the kitchen, she gave me a hug and told me two things: I love you. Dinner is at seven.

I came upstairs and took a long shower, and when I came out of the bathroom just now, I saw the red dress hanging on the closet door. I sat and stared at it for the longest time. The hospital room seems very far away somehow—like a dream.

Was I really just there?

Did I really collapse?

Was it really because I've been dieting?

All I want is to fit in this dress. I started to get dressed, and then instead of pulling on my jeans, I walked over and took the dress off the hanger. I was able to zip it all the way up, and it's only a tiny bit snug. Three more pounds is all it would take.

I felt my heart begin to race, and for the first time in this whole ordeal, a tear slid down my cheek. I thought about Jack's face when I walked down the stairs in this dress. I'm three pounds away from that moment.

I don't want to end up back in the hospital. I don't want to be locked up on the psych floor. Why is it so wrong for me to want my body to be perfect?

I've come so far. I can't stop now, can I?

Mom just called up the stairs. Dinner is ready.

Monday, October 1
Weight: 114

I thought it would be all over school today, but if anyone had heard about me passing out during the race on Saturday, no one seemed that interested.

Except for Vanessa.

She met me in the parking lot this morning. As I pulled in, she walked toward my car, and I let out a long, slow sigh. I didn't think I could handle an "I told you so" this early in the day, but it looked like I wouldn't have a choice. I grabbed my bag, climbed out of the SUV, and braced myself for her scolding.

Instead, she gave me a hug.

Vanessa: I'm so glad you're okay. I was so scared.

It was Vanessa who got to me first. Vanessa who stopped running to roll me over and make sure I was still breathing. Now she was crying and hugging me, and instead of feeling her disapproval, all I felt was her love. We stood and cried in the parking lot.

Vanessa: I don't want to lose you.

Me: You won't.

Vanessa: I won't lie for you anymore. If your food diary isn't correct, I'm going to tell Coach. I'm going to speak up because I won't stand by while you starve yourself to death.

I followed her to the bathroom, where we fixed our makeup. I looked at her in the mirror and whispered, "Thank you."

Vanessa: For what?

Me: For being my friend.

She smiled, then we grabbed our stuff and hurried to first period. Jill was quiet all morning between classes, and went off

193

campus with Rob for lunch. I texted her and she texted me back to say she'd call me tonight after her ballet class.

I wonder if she's worried. I can't help thinking that maybe she's afraid I'll tell people how much she's been restricting her calories. I would never do that to her. Her body is her business. Maybe she's not worried about me telling anyone else. Maybe she's worried I won't be as fun to hang out with? Or that I'll get preachy like Vanessa? I know I just need to talk to her so that she'll know I'm still the same old me, even if I have to eat more.

I checked in with Coach at practice and told her what I'd had for lunch: turkey wrap, apple, half a bag of fruit snacks. She hugged me too, and all of a sudden when she did, I just wanted to get out of there. I knew she wasn't going to let me run, but I resent having to tell her what I ate for lunch. The thought went through my head that I wished everyone would stop hugging me. Jill didn't hug me today. She kept her distance. She probably knew I needed some space.

Jill still gets me better than anybody else.

Except maybe Jack.

We talked on the phone last night after dinner, and I told him I wasn't allowed to practice until I'd fully recovered. I did not go into what "fully recovered" entailed. I didn't want him to think his girlfriend was going to become a blimp. He came by after his soccer practice just now. His hair was all sweaty and he was wearing soccer sandals and those big socks that normally go over your shin guards.

There is something undeniably sexy about a boy in soccer socks. We made out for a while on the couch, and then he just held me and we watched TV. Or I should say, the TV was on.

Jack: You okay?

Me: I will be.

Jack: Is there anything I can do?

Me: You're doing it.

I felt his big biceps tense around me as he squeezed me gently to his chest. I kicked him out at 7 p.m., when I knew Mom was clocking out at the hospital.

Jack: I liked it better when your mom worked nights.

Me: You and me both.

Wednesday, October 3
Weight: I DON'T KNOW

I don't *know* how much I weigh right now because Mom threw the scale away. She literally put it out with the trash yesterday morning. I weighed myself yesterday morning before school, then drove off to endure *another* day of Jill being standoffish, Vanessa being wildly huggy, and Coach making me recite what I had for lunch when I checked in at practice.

As I was driving home, it hit me: I'm cranky because I haven't been running. I have been missing my runner's high. My brain needs those chemicals to deal with stress. Of course, Mom and Coach would flip if they knew I'd started running again, but I'm so close to fitting in the dress, and I've been eating every single meal every single day since Sunday night.

I changed and did a quick four-mile loop around the neighborhood, then showered and stashed my shoes in my closet instead of leaving them by the back door like I usually do. I was working on chemistry when Mom got back from work.

She poked her head in my room and started asking me about my day, then started giving me the third degree about what I'd done after school.

Me: You're looking at it. Chemistry.

Mom: Have you talked to Jill?

Me: I saw her at school today. She's at ballet.

Mom: She called you Monday night, right?

Me: Yeah, on her way home from class.

Mom: And?

Me: And . . . what?

Mom: Honey, I'm just . . . worried.

Me: Worried about what?

Mom: I want you to be careful about hanging out with Jill.

I lost my mind. I yelled. Mom yelled back. I started crying. I told her Jill was my best friend and I didn't care. I was going to hang out with her. Mom brought up Susan, and how she was encouraging Jill to get too thin for ballet and how dangerous that was, and the longer I listened the more quiet I became. Sometimes when I get mad at Mom I just shut down.

This was one of those times.

She finally finished lecturing me and I took several deep breaths. When I heard her go back downstairs and start pulling food out of the fridge, I went to the bathroom to weigh myself. I don't know why, but it calms me down, knowing for sure what my weight is. Somehow the knowing makes it okay—makes it all measurable and manageable. It gives things an order, a number, a plan of action.

The scale was gone.

Sometimes Mom has borrowed it to weigh boxes when she sends something she's bought online back because it doesn't fit. I walked into her room and looked by her desk. It wasn't there either. I checked her bathroom. No luck. Finally I went downstairs and asked her where it was.

Mom: I threw it away, sweetheart.

Me: You *what*?

It came out louder and more shrill than I'd intended it to.

Mom: You are obsessed about how much you weigh and it's

not healthy. You were in the *hospital* on Saturday and Sunday because you're not *eating enough*.

Suddenly we were shouting again. I kept screaming about how I was supposed to make sure I was eating enough calories, how I would know if it was working. She kept saying how unhealthy it was until finally I'd had it.

Me: Unhealthy? I'm the unhealthy one? Have you looked at yourself in the mirror lately?

Mom: That's *it*, young lady. You're *grounded*.

Me (laughing): Grounded? From what? The *scale*?

Mom: You are not to leave this house without my permission. You are not to talk to or hang out with Jill unless you tell me about it. And no dates with Jack for a week.

Me: Fine. I'll go stay at Dad's for a week.

Mom: Oh no, you won't.

Me: Watch me.

Thursday, October 4
Weight: 115.5

I've gained almost two pounds since Sunday, but at least I know about it. This morning Mom left for work with strict instructions that I go directly to school and then come directly home. I smiled and nodded.

I drove directly to Jill's and texted her from the driveway.

She appeared at the front door and raised her hand to wave with a timid smile. I ran up the sidewalk.

Me: I need to use your scale.

Jill: I was afraid something like this might be happening at your house.

Me: You don't want to know.

Jill: I'll bet I can guess. Your scale disappeared, huh?

And just like that, we were back to normal. The swell of relief that started when I saw her smile at the front door flooded through me completely when I stepped onto the clear glass square in the corner of her bathroom and watched the cool blue glow of the digital numbers scramble up to . . . 115.5. I groaned.

Jill: Not so bad. At least you know. They pumped you full of all kinds of sugar water in the hospital.

Me: I only have two weeks before homecoming. I have to be at 110 for that dress to fit.

Jill: Five pounds is nothing. You're fine. You can't give up now.

Me: But I have to eat every single meal my mother puts on the table.

Jill: Do you?

I just blinked at her. She was right. I was standing in her house, hanging out with her even though Mom didn't want me to. I was using the scale even though Mom didn't want me to. I could eat or not eat whatever I wanted. What my mom wants or doesn't want really isn't my problem.

Jill saw the lightbulb go off in my head, and I smiled for what felt like the first time in days.

Jill: Welcome back.

I lay on her bed and we talked about how things were going in ballet for her. Classes had taken on a pretty competitive edge with Misty Jenkins always trying to outdo her now that casting for *The Nutcracker* had been handed down. When Jill was ready, we walked downstairs. Susan blew us kisses in the hallway as she sailed out the door in a trim navy business suit with an attaché case.

Jack was eating Lucky Charms at the island in the kitchen, and a big smile spread across his face when he saw me.

Jack: What are you doing here?

Me: Had to talk to your sister.

Jill: Confidential BFF assistance was required, *mon frère*.

He gulped down the pinkish milk at the bottom of his cereal bowl, then put his dishes in the sink and pulled me in for a kiss.

Jack: Wish I could wake up and have you here every morning.

It was the best start to a school day I'd had in a long time. I did well on my chemistry test in third period, and when I turned my phone on between classes, I had a voice mail from Dad:

Sure! I'd love for you to spend the weekend. Come over Friday night. I'll be home by eight, and we can go see a movie, or get food, or whatever you want.

Sunday, October 7
Weight: 114.5

Just got back from Dad's place. It was wildly depressing. He's living in this really nice condo not far from the dealership. It's full of new furniture that's comfortable, but it looks like he walked into a Crate and Barrel and just pointed at a sectional and chairs and beds and lamps and end tables. Also, there is n-o-t-h-i-n-g on the walls, which makes it feel sort of barren.

We went shopping to get bedding for the guest room where I slept. He had a bed already, but we had to go buy sheets and a comforter and pillows. He pulled out his Amex and kept asking me if I needed anything else, like if he just bought enough stuff for the guest room it would be more comfortable and might also ease the discomfort between us.

Dad: What else do you need?
Me: Well, there's no toothbrush holder in the bathroom.
We wheeled into the bathroom section and chose bath

accessories: soap dispenser and hand soap, a toothbrush holder, shower caddy, bath mat. I slipped a scale into the cart as well. He didn't blink.

Afterward, we went to dinner, just us this time. I ordered a soup and salad combo. Dad sent several text messages, and I assume they were to Annette. She probably thinks I hate her or something. I don't.

Last night, I asked Dad if Jack and Jill and Rob could meet us for a movie.

Dad: Your mom called me and said you're grounded. What'd you do?

Me: I told her I wasn't going to stop hanging out with Jill.

Dad: Why does she want you to do that?

Me: She thinks Jill is convincing me to starve myself.

Dad: Are you starving yourself?

Me: No! I just run a lot.

Dad: I know a lot of people who run a lot who don't wind up in the hospital.

Me: I'm fine. You saw me eat dinner.

In the end he relented. Jack met us at the theater with Jill and Rob. Annette met Dad. She smiled at me tentatively. I smiled back and gave her a polite hello. The movie was based on a book for teenagers about (surprise) teenagers. It was sort of a love story and sort of a story about a guy who is really depressed trying to figure out why. There are three main friends and they go riding around in a pickup truck listening to music. They take turns standing in the back of the truck as they drive through a tunnel in Pittsburgh, and at one point the main boy says, "We are infinite."

I don't know why, but that part made me cry. Big tears slid down my cheeks and I tried to be sneaky when I reached up to wipe them away, but Jack saw. You know what I like best about Jack? He didn't ask why I was crying, he just reached over and laid his hand on my leg, and I wove my fingers through his, and we sat like that until the movie was over.

This afternoon, I packed up all my stuff and came home while Mom was still at work. It gave me a chance to go for a run before she got home and also to stash the new scale Dad bought under my bed.

When Mom got home it was like nothing had happened last week—like we never fought. Maybe she got the message. Or maybe she's afraid of losing me. Whatever the reason, she brought home Thai food and called me downstairs. We sat on the couch and she ate curry while I pretended to, and we watched TV.

I'm heading to bed now so I can get up early in the morning and run before school. Mom will probably not be pleased, but I don't care. I've got almost two weeks before homecoming.

Thursday, October 11
Weight: 112.5

Only two more pounds to go. I've been eating nothing but lettuce at lunch, and Vanessa told me today she's going to turn me in to Coach Perkins tomorrow. I opened my mouth to answer but nothing came out. As I turned to walk away, she grabbed my arm.

Me: Let go of me.

Vanessa: *No!* I won't just let go of you. I don't want you to die.

Me: You are such a drama queen. I'm not dying.

Vanessa: I'm telling Coach.

Me: Okay.

Vanessa: Okay what?

Me: Okay fine. Tell Coach. I just don't care. I don't have the energy to fight with you about this.

Vanessa: She's going to kick you off the team.

Me: Yes, she probably will.

Vanessa: And you're just *okay* with that? We could win at *state* this year.

Me: Not without me you won't.

All of my clothes are really baggy on me now. My breasts have gotten smaller and a lot of my shirts don't fit the way they used to. I don't really fill them out anymore. Luckily, it's cooler

now, and I've pulled out some of my cardigans and hoodies.
When I wear long sleeves and baggier tops over leggings and
jeans it's harder to tell that I'm a lot skinnier. Mom even saw me
this morning in the kitchen and said I looked really nice before
she ran out the door to work. She's going out with Pam tonight.
Some sort of speed-dating thing Pam signed her up for. She's all
excited about it.

At least she won't be here for dinner. I'm so tired of spitting
food into napkins. Also, if I have to drink one more mug of that
tea Jill gave me I might dissolve completely.

I just finished the workout Jill showed me, and I'm going
to go on a quick run before Mom comes home from work. That
should burn off about two-thirds of the 1,200 calories I've had
so far today.

Friday, October 12
Weight: 112

Coach Perkins told me I was benched for the rest of the season
unless I bring my weight up. There were tears in her eyes when
she told me. She's going to call Mom to talk to her about "the
situation." She announced to everybody that Vanessa would
be the new team captain for the time being. I don't care. That's
what Vanessa wanted anyway. I don't understand why everybody

thinks sports are so important in high school. It's not like any of us are going to run cross-country professionally one day. And when the rest of them stop running, they'll get fat.

Not me.

Just because I'm benched for another two weeks doesn't mean I'm going to stop running.

Saturday, October 13
Weight: 111.5

Jill and I met Vanessa and Geoff to watch Jack and Rob's soccer game last night before Mom got home from work. Afterward, we went to this ancient diner Rob loves called Rick's. It's a greasy spoon attached to an old hotel. There's a ceiling fan over every table and you can tell from the color of the ceiling tiles that people used to sit in there and chain-smoke.

Our favorite waitress, Marlene, was wearing her signature metallic blue eye shadow. She sat us back in the corner booth, where Rob and Jack immediately ordered chicken-fried steak with gravy. Vanessa and Geoff got chocolate malts, and Jill and I both sipped hot water and lemon, and split a chef's salad—dressing on the side. The guys have been finalizing plans for homecoming next week, and they are so cute when they talk about it.

Jill told me she wants to see me in the dress and told me that she found the perfect shoes to go with it. I told her we'd have to figure out a time for her to come over while my mom was gone.

When I got home, Mom was really upset. She'd been crying and trying to call me. I had turned off my phone because I figured she'd hit the roof when she got the message from Coach.

She did.

Instead of getting angry with her, I just slowly and calmly walked upstairs to my room and started to get undressed. She followed me, warning and pleading, yelling and crying. As she did, I quietly pulled the dress out of its plastic bag and slipped it off the hanger. I slowly slipped one leg into it, and then the other. The light, slick fabric of the silk lining whispered over my thighs and hips. As I slid my arms into the sleeves, Mom began begging me to talk to her, begging me to be honest with her.

Mom: What is it that you want? What do you *need* from me?

Me: I need you to zip me up.

I turned my back to her, holding my hair up out of the way with one arm, while the other held the front of the dress across my chest. I watched in the mirror as she snapped out of her crying jag and really saw me for the first time since I'd gotten home. She realized that I was finally trying on the dress for her.

Slowly, she reached forward and slid the zipper up. I grabbed a hair clip and wound my hair up in a loose twist, then dropped my arms and pushed up on my tiptoes like I had done for Susan and Jill in the dressing room and took a step back from the mirror. The dress fit perfectly.

Mom gasped.

I glanced at her in the mirror, and her eyes were wide, like she was seeing a vision. She opened her mouth to say something, then closed it, then for the first time since I'd gotten home she spoke without sounding angry.

Mom: That dress . . . you look . . .

Me: Amazing. I look amazing.

We stood there staring at my reflection in the mirror for a moment.

Mom: You look like something out of a magazine.

After a minute or so, Mom sank down on the edge of my bed, and I slipped the dress off and back onto the hanger.

Me: This is all I wanted. I just wanted to look beautiful for Jack. Can you understand that?

Mom: Sweetheart, you were beautiful enough for Jack before you lost all this weight. It's getting dangerous now.

Me: Just let me have this one night. I just want a perfect homecoming dance, and then you can stuff me full of burgers and french fries. I promise.

I sat down on the bed next to her, and Mom put both arms around me.

Mom: I'm scared. I don't know how to help you.

Me: I don't need any help.

Mom: That's what scares me the most.

I've been thinking about why she said that. I've been wondering why she would be scared that I don't think I need any help. It makes me angry that she can't see what I've accomplished with my body. It makes me feel like throwing things at the wall that she could see me in that dress and tell me I look like something out of a magazine and not be *thrilled*. How could looking that beautiful ever be a problem?

Jill's coming over to pick me up and we're going to go buy the shoes.

Sunday, October 14
Weight: 111

Mom let Jill sleep over last night. I think she's decided that she can't keep me from hanging out with Jill, so she might as well keep both of us under her watchful eye. I don't know what it is she thinks she can stop by being in the same house with us, but I didn't try to figure this out. Sometimes my mother baffles me completely.

Jill was right about the shoes. They're silver heels with a slightly rounded toe and crystals embedded in a ring around a thick heel. They look like a souped-up version of something Marilyn Monroe would have worn. Something about them says old-school glamour just like the dress, and when I walk you can just barely see the silver toe flash through the drape of the skirt in the front. Jill was as loud as Mom was speechless when I slipped into the dress for the first time. She squealed and jumped up and down like she had when she got cast as Clara. She insisted on taking a picture to post on the website.

Jill: You have to provide some inspiration for all the other girls on the forum.

Me: I don't know. I'm not sure I want my face on the Internet.

Jill: I'll crop out your face. Oh! Or better yet, look over your shoulder and I'll take it from an angle where we can only see your hair.

Jill snapped the picture on her phone, then loaded it into an app and chose a filter that made the color wash out in the center just bit. She added a textured white frame that made the whole image appear to be a snapshot from the 1940s or '50s.

Jill: You look like a legend of the silver screen.

I blushed and giggled, then we logged on to the forum, and

Jill registered as a new user for me. After some debate we settled on a username: weigh2go. She posted the photo and underneath it wrote these words:

"Don't think about how hungry you are. Think about how skinny you're getting."

She tagged the picture "thinspiration."

Wednesday, October 17
Weight: 110

I hate myself right now.

Everything was going great today. Got up this morning and did a hard forty five-minute run. I weighed in a pound lighter than I was on Sunday, then ate an egg, a plum, and a spoonful of peanut butter for breakfast. At lunch I only had a salad, and then Mom grilled fish for dinner and I had a few pieces of broccoli. Then I was upstairs doing my homework and I smelled it: cookies.

I went downstairs to the kitchen, and Mom was taking out two giant silver baking sheets of homemade chocolate chip cookies—just like she used to make for me when I was a little girl on the last day of school.

Mom: Thought you might need a study break.

Me: Mom! You know I have homecoming in three days.

Mom: Oh, c'mon. One cookie is not going to kill you.

I couldn't *stop myself.* I *had* to eat one. The chocolate chips were all warm and gooey. The cookie melted on my tongue, and when I opened my eyes after the first bite, Mom was standing there holding a frosty glass of milk.

I ate *six.* I am such a fatty fatso. They were delicious, but I can't stop thinking about it now. I can almost feel my stomach growing as I write this. I hate myself for not being strong.

I just went onto the website a few minutes ago and posted about it. Jill must've seen it, because I got a text:

Jill: Cookies????

Me: I might throw up.

Jill: COOKIES???

Me: I know. I feel like total crap.

She called me after that and we talked. She suggested that I make a "Do This Instead" jar. This sounded like a great idea. I found an old shoe-box downstairs from my running shoes and I got some wrapping paper out of the hall closet and wrapped the box and the lid in bright solid red. Then I took a Sharpie and wrote "Do This Instead" in big, bold letters across the front.

I tore three sheets of paper out of my notebook and wrote out other things to do besides eating:

- Take a nap/go to bed early.
- Practice my Spanish.
- Text Jill for help.
- Look at "thinspiring" blogs online
- Really look at yourself in the mirror and remember *why* you're doing this.
- Read a book.
- Take a nice bubble bath.
- Read a book in a nice bubble bath.
- Weigh yourself and see how far you've come.
- Try on your tightest clothes.
- Go for a run.
- Research colleges.
- Do your cardio workout.
- Watch a movie.
- Write a note to slip in Jack's locker tomorrow.

I felt a little better when I was done, but I still made a mug of Jill's special ballerina tea. I posted a picture of my "Do This Instead" box on the forum. Jill saw it and posted right back:

Way to go, weigh2go!

It made me smile and hate myself a little less. We're going to have so much fun at homecoming.

Friday, October 19
Weight: 110

Tomorrow's the big day. Jill and Vanessa and I are meeting each other for mani/pedis tomorrow morning, and then we're going to Susan's stylist to get our hair and makeup done. Jill didn't want Vanessa to come.

Jill: After what she did to you with the whole cross-country thing, I don't know how you can stand her.

Me: It's not that big a deal. She didn't do this. I did this. I look better than I ever have.

Jill (sighing): I guess it won't hurt to have her in the pictures. It will give everyone else a point of reference for how thin and gorgeous we look.

Jill said Jack had already picked out my corsage. I actually bounced up and down on the bed.

Me: Please please please tell me he got roses and it's for my wrist.

Jill: Are you kidding? Like Mom would let him ruin the neckline of that dress. Yes. White roses, no baby's breath, wrist corsage.

Me: Is it pretty?

Jill: If it looks like the picture of the one he showed me on his phone, it's perfect.

Mom insisted that the limo come by our place so she can take pictures at our house instead of me going over to Jill's. I'm glad she did. It will be fun to walk down our big staircase in this dress and see the look on Jack's face.

Sunday, October 21
Weight: Don't know

The look on Jack's face when he picked me up for the dance was priceless. Dad had stopped by to take pictures, too. He and Mom have been talking again since they saw each other at the hospital after that race where I went down. Anyway, Jack was in midsentence joking around with Dad. When he saw me, his voice trailed off, and he just stared. I'd practiced walking down the stairs four or five times before he got there so I wouldn't trip on the dress or break my ankle in the heels. I felt like a model— a superstar. I took his breath away.

It wasn't the only time that it happened that night.

The limo was so long we could've fit twelve more people in it. Rob somehow managed to sneak a bottle of champagne under his jacket and Jack had another one stashed under the seat. Everyone but Vanessa had a glass on the way to the school, but thankfully, she didn't make a big deal out of it. She did roll her eyes when Geoff poured a second glass for himself, but who can blame him? He probably needed a third glass just to deal with her attitude. The driver dropped us off at the door, and Rob and Jack agreed on a time when he should come back to pick us up.

When we got out of the car, I wobbled just a little, then giggled. The bubbles and sugar had gone straight to my head. Jack offered me his arm and was the perfect gentleman for the entire dance. He never left my side for a second. We turned heads everywhere we walked, and girls who had never spoken to me in the halls for the past two years stopped me to tell me how beautiful my dress was. We danced for hours, and I was amazed that my feet didn't hurt in these heels. I guess you get what you pay for.

I got dizzy after a couple of hours, but I decided it must just be the champagne, and besides, I had the best-looking date at the dance (even if Rob was named homecoming king). After a while the band slowed things down, and I just leaned into Jack while we danced. I could feel him pressed up against me, and his breath on my ear sent goose bumps running down my arms.

Jack: Are you cold?

Me: No. You just do that to me.

Jack: Do you have any idea what you're doing to me tonight in that dress?

Me: I think I can feel what I'm doing to you.

Jack: Just a little?

Me: It's not so little.

He winked at me and smirked, but he was blushing. Hard.

Not long after that, Rob declared that it was time to hit the after-party. One of their friends on the soccer team had rented a room at an old hotel that used to be the estate of a movie star. Now it was a resort with three swimming pools and lush grounds where you could lie in a hammock or play a game of croquet, all with a view of the mountains.

Geoff and Rob broke open the second bottle of champagne and Jack and I shared another glass while Rob told the driver he needed a burger. We wound up taking the limo into the drive-through. My head was so buzzy from the champagne and I got really hungry all of a sudden. Not just hungry: ravenous. Jack asked me if I wanted anything, and I opened my mouth to tell him yes, but Jill caught my eye and gave me a look.

Me: I'll just have a couple of your fries.

Jack: You sure?

Me: Yeah, I'm good.

Jill looked at me across the limo and mouthed the words "stay strong." I smiled at her as Jack ordered, and mouthed back "thank you."

I should have eaten those fries. I wish I had ordered a whole value meal and a chocolate milk shake for myself. If I had, I wouldn't be writing this from a hospital bed on the thirteenth floor.

I still can't remember exactly what happened. I remember pulling up to the high front wall of the hotel. I remember the valets in salmon-colored pants opening the limo. I remember Jack stepping out of the car then turning back to offer me his hand. I remember stepping out of the car and the breeze on my cheek. I remember turning toward the tall, orange doors of the hotel lobby and walking through them on Jack's arm. The entire hotel has been designed in this retro 1960s glamour-puss style, and there are two suits of armor guarding the bathroom doors by the front desk. I remember thinking that Jack was my knight in shining armor, and I was about to tell him as we walked by the mod round fire pit by the back door, but the next thing I knew, I was lying on a couch by the door, and everyone was on their phones, except Jack.

Jack: Hey, babe. Are you with me? Can you hear me?

I tried to sit up and he gently took my hand and laid me back down.

Jack: I'm right here. I'm not going anywhere.

Me: I . . . I'm fine.

Jack: My dad is on his way.

When he said that, I got scared. If parents were involved, this was not going to be the night I had wanted. I'm not sure why I yelled at Jack. I think it was because I was scared.

Me: Why did you do that? God!

I pushed myself up on the couch. I tried to stand up but fell forward. I slipped through Jack's arm and hit my chin on the coffee table next to the couch. Blood was everywhere. Vanessa screamed; Jill ran between the two suits of armor and came back with paper towels. The hotel manager was there asking if I was drunk, and at that moment Jack's dad walked in. I don't remember what he said to Geoff or Rob, or Jill or Vanessa. I don't remember how he talked the hotel manager out of calling the police.

All I remember is Jack.

Holding me.

And crying.

Jack held me in the backseat of his dad's car all the way to the hospital. When we walked through the doors of the ER, every single head in the waiting room turned to stare, and I realized we were still wearing formal clothes. Jack slid off his tux jacket and draped it over my shoulders.

At that moment, Mom came through the doors from the parking lot into the waiting area. She stopped short at the sight of us standing there, me with blood pooling in a paper towel at my chin. She held up a finger to James, then disappeared through the double doors into the emergency room. James turned back to Jack and me. He had the kindest smile.

James: Everything's going to be okay.

Me: Everything's fine now. I don't think this cut is bad.

James nodded, and Jack held on to my shoulders as an orderly came back with my mom and a wheelchair, and Dr. Nash.

Me: I don't need that wheelchair.

Mom: Sweetheart, don't make this any worse than it is.

I turned to look at Jack. His eyes were red and glossy from tears, but he smiled and said one word.

Please.

Something about that word made me feel so tired, like I could fall asleep standing up. I nodded at him and let him help me into the wheelchair. He got down on his knees in front of me and said three more words:

I love you.

Then the orderly handed him his jacket and wheeled me away.

I passed out one more time after they got me onto a gurney in the back and started an IV. When I came to, Dr. Nash was talking to my mom:

Dehydrated

Overexercise

Her body is in a famine mode

Drastically restricted fats to the point that her liver is shutting down

Thirteenth floor

When I woke up this morning, Mom was sitting in my room. I tried to reach up and wipe the sleep out of my eye, but I felt something tighten around my wrist. I looked down and saw restraints. I looked at Mom, and she was crying.

Me: What the *hell*, Mom? Why am I *tied up* like a *crazy person*?

Mom: Oh, honey. You kept waking up and trying to pull the IV out of your arm.

Me: What is in this IV?

Mom: It's fluids and nutrients.

I knew what that meant. It meant they were pumping me full of sugar water. I couldn't help myself. I started shouting.

Me: You are pumping me full of calories! Of course I want to pull it out. You tell them to take it out of my arm this second. Don't you see what you're doing? I'm going to get so fat just lying here. Is that what you *want*? It *is* what you want, isn't it? You *want* me to be *fat and miserable* just like *YOU*.

I was out of breath, and Mom was sobbing, saying, "No," and "Oh, honey," over and over again. She stood up and I saw she had something in her hands. It was a mirror. She held it up to my face. I closed my eyes and turned my head away.

Me: *No!* I don't want to see how *fat* I'm getting. I don't want to see what the sugar you're pumping me full of has already done to my face.

She cried, but she wouldn't go away, and she wouldn't move the mirror. Finally, I turned to look into it.

Mom: Can't you see it? Your hair is getting thin and breaking off. Your cheeks are so hollow. Your eyes don't even shine anymore. Your skin is gray. Where is she? Look in this mirror and find my sweet girl! Where did she go? You're starving her to death.

As I looked in the mirror, I realized I didn't know when the last time was I'd actually looked myself in the eyes. I was always too busy looking at my body, checking for places that should be flatter or more toned. My eyes seemed dull and gray. Hadn't they been blue once? I stared until I didn't recognize myself anymore. The only way I knew it was me I was looking at was when I saw the tears start to fall, and I felt them, hot and wet, trickling down my cheeks.

Tuesday, October 23
Weight: 112

They released me this morning. Mom's insurance won't allow me to stay there for longer than seventy two hours without being sent to long-term treatment. Dr. Nash said if I don't start eating again, she'll make sure I get locked up for twenty eight days.

I hate her.

I want to text Jack and tell him I'm okay. I want to text Jill and ask her what I should do next. Mom won't let me have my phone back yet.

I hate her, too.

Wednesday, October 24
Weight: 113

This is a nightmare. Mom still wouldn't let me go to school today. She's taken some vacation days from work, too. Jack stopped by after soccer practice today. He brought me flowers. Gerbera daisies. Red this time. Mom invited him in and called me downstairs. Was it only five days ago I walked down the stairs to meet him and felt like a movie star? When I saw it was him, I wanted to run back up to my room. I stopped on the stairs for a second. Everybody just waited. I was staring at my feet, and then I started to cry. I didn't want him to see me like this. I guess I know in my head somewhere that I'm not really fat, but I *feel* so fat and ugly right now. I have stitches in my chin. I've been pumped full of crap at the hospital.

Jack set the flowers on the island and walked up the steps

toward me. Mom followed him and stood at the foot of the stairs in the living room. He wrapped his arm around me like I was fragile and might break in two if he squeezed too hard. Something about being close to him made me feel safe, and I leaned into the soft skin of his neck and just cried.

Jack: What is it, babe?

Me: I don't want you to see me like this.

Jack: You look amazing to me. I haven't seen you since Saturday night. That's way too long. I've been jonesing.

How does he know how to say the right thing every time? He turned to my mom.

Jack: Do you think it'd be okay if we took a walk down to the park?

Mom: It would be totally fine, but we have to leave in about twenty minutes to get to the doctor.

Me: What? What doctor?

Mom: I made an appointment for us.

Me: For *us*?

Jack: It's okay, babe. I'll come back tomorrow.

He kissed me on the forehead and left before I could stop him or figure out from Mom where this appointment was. Turns out Mom has booked us with a shrink. I'm so pissed off right now I can barely hold the pen. I shouldn't be going to see a therapist, I should be going to school. I should be walking down the street right now with my boyfriend, holding his hand, hearing about his day.

I told Mom she was ruining my life. She told me if I don't go with her, I wasn't going back to school.

I'll do anything to not have to sit at home with her all day.

Later . . .

The car ride to the therapist's office was complete silence. Mom tried to talk, but then gave up. Thank God.

Of course, once we were in Dr. Crane's office she let the floodgates open and it all gushed out. Dr. Crane is this little bald guy who is probably in his forties. He has a nice smile and bright eyes, and he was really friendly. I think he might be gay. He's in remarkably good shape and wears very cool glasses. The lenses are rectangular and sort of disappear because they're frameless. I kept staring at his glasses, sort of blurring my eyes a little, seeing if I could make out the lenses at all while Mom cried her eyes out about how scared she was. How upset she felt that she couldn't stop me. How angry she was that I didn't see what I was doing to myself and to her and to my dad.

Dr. Crane: How do you feel about that?

Me: How do I feel about what?

Dr. Crane: All of the things your mother just said.

225

Me: I feel like I don't want to be here right now. I feel like I don't want to talk about this. It's none of anyone else's business.

Dr. Crane gave me his little friendly, bright-eyed smile. He nodded. Then he asked my mom if she would mind stepping out so he could have some time alone with me. Mom looked sort of bewildered, but she dried her eyes and left the room. I settled back into the deep cushions of the couch, and Dr. Crane asked if I wanted any water or anything. I told him no.

Dr. Crane: Is there anything you want to tell me that you'd rather your mom not hear?

Me: No.

Dr. Crane: Do you trust me?

Me: I've actually watched television before in my life, so yes, I am familiar with the idea that psychologists are generally trustworthy.

It surprised me when he laughed.

Dr. Crane: You're funny.

Me: I bet you think I'm too skinny, too.

Dr. Crane: I don't really care what you weigh.

Me: You're the only one, then. The rest of us just can't get enough of it.

Dr. Crane: Who is this friend Jill your mom talked about?

Me: She talked about Jill?

Dr. Crane: Yeah. You were sort of staring at me during that part. I wasn't sure if you were actually listening or not.

Me: Yeah, I wasn't. I was checking out your glasses. They're really cool.

Dr. Crane: Thank you.

Me: Jill is my friend.

Dr. Crane: Your mom is pretty upset. She just told me that she wishes she'd never let you hang out with Jill.

Me: Jill isn't making me do this.

Dr. Crane: Do what?

Me: Count calories. Lose weight.

Dr. Crane: Does Jill do those things too?

Me: Yes.

Dr. Crane: But it's not your disease that makes her your friend.

Me: My . . . disease?

Dr. Crane looked at me with eyes full of concern. It made me angry.

Dr. Crane: Yes. The reason you're here is the disease of anorexia.

Me: I don't have a *disease*. I have *willpower*.

Dr. Crane flipped open a chart on the little glass table next to his chair.

Dr. Crane: What you have is a liver that is shutting down,

signs of scalp hair loss, elevated levels of serum sodium, potassium chloride, and carbon dioxide from continued dehydration, muscle wasting, and no regular period for months. Those are not signs of willpower. Those are symptoms of a disease called anorexia.

He said all this softly and gently, and then held my gaze as I sat there blinking at him.

Dr. Crane: Is anorexia what makes Jill your friend?

Me: No. Of course not. I'm not sure if she'll even want to be my friend anymore after this.

Dr. Crane: Why wouldn't she?

Me: She's got to do what's best for her. She's got to stay thin so she can be the best at ballet she can possibly be.

Dr. Crane: What other friends do you have? Your mother didn't mention anyone else by name.

I thought about telling him about Vanessa and Geoff and Rob and especially Jack. None of those names left my lips, though. When I opened my mouth, I didn't recognize my own voice.

Me: I feel like I am my best friend. When I'm able to get through a meal without eating too much, there's this thing I feel inside of me—this strength. It's like a place of power, and when I don't eat too much, or when I exercise enough, it makes me feel invincible. It keeps me company.

Dr. Crane: Your disease has become your best friend.

When he said those words, I couldn't speak anymore. I just looked at him, nodded, and cried.

Wednesday, November 7
Weight: 119

It's weird how two weeks can seem like two years. My life has been a completely different place since that night at homecoming. I've been seeing Dr. Crane three times each week. He runs an outpatient program for people with eating disorders at the hospital where Mom works. I go three days each week after school: Mondays, Tuesdays, and Thursdays.

On Tuesdays I see Dr. Crane one-on-one, and on Mondays and Thursdays, it's a "group therapy" session. Dr. Crane leads the conversation with seven or eight other girls. Most of us are in high school. Most of us are anorexic. A couple of the girls are bulimic and do a lot of bingeing and purging. A girl named Amy talked about eating a whole box of cupcakes, then making herself throw up. Just hearing her talk about it made me feel sick to my stomach.

This girl named Kim, who is a senior in Jack and Rob's class at school, is in the group. I was shocked to see somebody I knew there—especially her. She's a cheerleader and has big boobs and what Jill likes to call an "athletic spread," which means her butt and thighs are full and curvy. She doesn't look like she's missed a meal in quite a while. Today I found out that's because she hasn't. She's been what she calls "recovered" for three years.

Dr. Crane usually starts the group off with a topic. Today was about what we see when we look in the mirror. He calls it body image. When it was Kim's turn she said that she knows she needs to be careful when she gets too caught up in the mirror. She said that's when she knows her vision can start doing funky things.

Kim: Sometimes I catch myself staring at something in the mirror besides my eyes, and I know that's a trigger for me. I have to remind myself that I don't always see what's actually in the mirror.

Dr. Crane: Can you tell us a little bit more about that? What does it feel like?

Kim: Well, it used to be that I weighed about ninety-eight pounds, which meant for my height I was almost twenty-five pounds underweight, but I'd look in the mirror and see fat hanging over my waistband. I'd convince myself I had a muffin top, or that my thighs were too big under my cheerleading skirt.

Dr. Crane asked if anybody else had experienced this. Everybody in the circle raised a hand. Except me, at first.

When I saw everybody else's hand in the air, I sighed and put mine up too.

Dr. Crane smiled his little smile at me.

Afterward, Kim came up to say hi.

Kim: I'm glad you're here.

Me: I can't say that I am.

Kim: It gets better, I promise.

Me: I can't believe you aren't scared all the time.

Kim: Scared of what?

Me: Of becoming one of those girls that can't control how much she eats.

Kim smiled at me, a sad smile—almost like she could see something about me that I couldn't.

Kim: Just keep coming to group. It gets easier.

She gave me her cell phone number, and I typed it into my contacts, but I can't imagine actually talking to her about anything. When I think about Kim and her big boobs and the way her thighs touch when she walks, I get this sick feeling in the pit of my stomach. I have to take deep breaths so I don't gag. She just seems revolting to me.

I've gained three pounds each week since I got out of the hospital. Dr. Nash says I'm still fifteen pounds under my goal weight. I have a checkup with her once a week too. I told her I couldn't eat any more than I was.

Dr. Nash: You can, it'll just take time for your body to readjust. You'll know you're back on track when you get your period again. Should be in the next seven to ten pounds.

The idea of weighing ten more pounds totally freaks me out.

Dr. Crane: Why does it freak you out?

Me: I don't want to be ugly.

Dr. Crane: What if you were *more* beautiful because you were at a healthy weight? Not less.

Me: But I won't be. Jack is always saying how perfect I look.

Dr. Crane: Have you seen Jack lately? Since you put back on six pounds?

Me: Yeah.

Dr. Crane: When?

Me: He came over for dinner last night.

Dr. Crane: Did he act any differently around you?

I thought about this for a minute. Mom had made us spaghetti and meatballs. I only ate a little bit of pasta, but I had three meatballs and a slice of French bread with garlic butter on it. Jack had laughed and joked and slurped noodles in this way that made me giggle.

After dinner we hung out on the sectional in the living room reading our books for English class. He's halfway through *A Tale of Two Cities* and I'm finishing up *Little Women*. He didn't seem any different at all. In fact, he was actually smiling more than usual.

Dr. Crane smiled when I told him this.

Dr. Crane: Jack loves you. Your mom loves you. Let them love you while you learn how to love yourself.

Me: But what if Jack stops? What if he . . .

Dr. Crane: Leaves?

I nodded.

Dr. Crane: People break up sometimes. Even when they're married like your mom and dad. It happens all the time. You can't control that by controlling what you eat. I can't promise you Jack won't leave. I *can* promise you he won't leave because you weren't thin or beautiful enough.

Sunday, November 11
Weight: 121

Geoff and Vanessa came over tonight with Jack. I invited Jill, too, but she's been in rehearsals for *The Nutcracker* every waking moment she's not at school. I want to believe that's why I haven't been hearing from her as much, and why she's been so quiet at school, but I know it's because I've been eating more again.

I feel like I've lost two friends in a way—restricting my calories, and Jill. It used to be that we were friends for lots of reasons. Now it seems like we were only friends for one reason. Kim was talking about that at group on Thursday, and it made a lot of sense to me.

Geoff and Jack insisted on ordering a pizza with jalapeños on it, so Vanessa and I got one with just Canadian bacon and pineapple on it. Geoff and Jack got into a pepper-eating contest to see who could handle the most and both of them ended up red in the face with tears running down their cheeks.

I was laughing so hard with Vanessa that my stomach actually hurt, and all of a sudden, I realized what a good time I was having. I hadn't laughed like that in a really long time. It reminded me of how easy things used to be between Vanessa and Geoff and me. I want it to be like that again, but I get scared that it might not ever be. Even while I was eating delicious pizza there was this little voice in the back of my head saying: *You are disgusting. You are a fatty fatso. You should hate yourself.*

I was able to shut it out and not think about it when everybody was there. After they went home it was a different story. I was up in my room, and I saw my red "Do This Instead" box. Suddenly I didn't want to be alone in my room anymore. I grabbed that box and the scale from under the bed, and I went to find Mom. I gave her both things.

She hugged me really tight for a long time, and then asked if I wanted to join her. We're sitting on her bed right now. She's reading a book while I write. I feel really close to her right now—like being honest was a good thing. She told me that we'd keep the scale in the front bathroom, and as long as I was eating, we'd weigh in every day. It feels weird to bring someone else into the bathroom with me to weigh myself, but Dr. Crane has been talking about that in our sessions. He thinks it's one more way that I can ask for help, that I can admit I am not in control of my food. He's been helping me see how it's the other way around—that food has actually been in control of *me*.

Wednesday, November 14
Weight: 122

I felt really crappy this morning when I woke up. Mom and I did our little weigh-in in the bathroom, and then I took a shower and started to get dressed. The skinny jeans I bought with Jill before school started are a little snug now, and I had to take them off and wear a pair of my older jeans. Mom poked her head in the door and saw me just staring at the skinny jeans lying on the bed. She walked over and put an arm around me.

Mom: Let's go shopping after school today?

I nodded. My heart was racing like it might explode. I felt all panicky, and I think Mom felt me shaking because she pulled me in really close and held me tight.

Mom: Sssh. Sweetheart, it's okay. It just means you're *healthy* again. You're getting there. You look so much better than you did six weeks ago.

After she left, I kept looking in the mirror, trying to keep my eyes on my eyes like Dr. Crane talks about doing. Trying to take in the whole of myself, instead of just the physical part. I *know* on some level deep inside that I look *better*—that I don't look sick anymore. But I get so angry when I see magazines at the grocery store or Jill walking through the halls. How come those girls are able to be that skinny, and I can't be?

Dr. Crane calls it an "inside job." Meaning that my problems—the stuff that I have been trying to control by not eating—aren't actually anybody else's actions. It's my own thinking that has to change.

Kim stopped by the lunch table where I was to say hi today. Jill was sitting next to Rob and got this look on her face like she was really amused. I tried to ignore it, but after Kim left, I was cutting up the pieces of chicken in my salad and caught Jill staring at me. My face flushed, and I felt this hot flash of anger shoot through me.

Me: *What?*

Jill shrugged and started gathering her stuff to leave. Jack looked at Jill with a thunderstorm on his face, and the air around the table got really tense. He had a warning in his voice when he said Jill's name.

Jill: Oh, butt out, Mr. Perfect.

Rob: Whoa. What's going on?

I was trying not to cry, but it wasn't any use. I felt Vanessa reach under the table and squeeze my leg. That made me even more frustrated. I didn't want to have to choose between my friends.

Me: I have to *eat*, Jill. I don't have a choice.

Jill: You always have a choice.

Jack jumped out of his chair and almost out of his skin. He pointed toward the cafeteria doors and said a single word in a very low voice:

Go.

Jill shook her head at me and walked away.

I know I should talk about this at group tomorrow, but I don't know if I can. I feel like my heart is breaking on the inside. I don't want to hurt Jill, but I can't go on hurting myself anymore, either.

Thursday, November 22
Weight: 125

We're at Grandma and Grandpa's today for Thanksgiving. I was just watching the Rockettes perform in the Macy's Thanksgiving Day Parade. Those girls have legs for days. It made me miss Jill. It also made me worried.

I went into Grandma's bathroom and found her scale. It's really old and still has a dial on the front—no digital numbers. It creaked and wobbled a little when I stepped onto it, but when the dial finally came to a rest from spinning back and forth it said 125. That means I've gained a full fifteen pounds since homecoming. I felt an old familiar panic descend over me like a fog rolling in. I texted Kim. She called me back right away.

Me: Help. Freaking out.

Kim: Turkey panic?

Me: I don't know. I was just watching the parade and I had to come weigh myself.

Kim: Ah. The Rockettes?

Me: How'd . . . how'd you know?

Kim: Lots of dancers are anorexic. Did you know those girls have weigh-ins?

Me: Really?

Kim: Yep. If they can't fit in their costumes, their understudy goes on.

Me: How am I going to make it through this meal?

Kim: Breathe. Remember that you have a disease that wants to control you.

Me: I'm ballooning up. I've gained fifteen pounds in six weeks!

Kim: That's normal. You're still underweight. Your body is repairing itself.

Me: I feel so fat and bloated. My stomach pooches out in the mirror.

Kim: That's your disease distorting your vision. You're still ten pounds underweight for your height.

Me: How are you so calm about this?

Kim: Because I've been at it for longer. You're doing everything just fine. You called me, didn't you?

I took a deep breath. Maybe Kim was right.

Me: What do I do?

Kim: You keep a journal, don't you?

Me: Yeah.

Kim: Write all of this down.

Me: How will that help?

Kim: Write down what you're feeling. Write down this conversation. If it doesn't help, call me back.

Me: Okay.

Kim: Remember, your feelings are important, but they're not facts. They'll change. Just give them ten minutes.

Me: Thanks, Kim.

I started writing the second I hung up. I wrote down that whole conversation, but I feel hopeless somehow. I know in my head that Kim is right, but I have this fear in my stomach that I'm going to become a monster. My nose is full of turkey and pumpkin pie right now, and any second Mom is going to call me to dinner and try to stuff me full of Grandma's mashed potatoes.

Maybe Kim is right. Just breathe. This is my disease talking. I don't have to eat the entire table, just a normal plateful. Try a bit of everything. It's like being a little girl again. *I hate this.*

Just for today, I won't restrict my calories. Maybe I'll do it tomorrow. I could always start again tomorrow and go back down to 1,000 per day. That idea makes me feel a little bit better. I don't have to eat like a hog forever, I'm just not going to count my calories for this one meal.

Jack just texted me:

Hey gorgeous. Thankful 4U.

I have to make sure he stays thankful and doesn't get repulsed.

Friday, November 23
Weight: 125

I had a meltdown at the mall just now.

Mom and Grandma love shopping Black Friday sales. Grandma has been making a big deal about how pretty I look now that I've "filled out" again. Even writing those words "filled out" makes me want to throw myself into traffic. It's like I'm a form, covered in somebody else's ideas of what I should look like. To make matters worse, Jack called last night and invited me to come see Jill do *The Nutcracker* on Saturday night. He said the whole family is really excited about it, and he wanted me to be his date.

When Mom heard this, she was determined to buy me a new outfit for the ballet, and Grandma was determined to pay for it. I should have just told them that the idea of shopping right now *terrifies* me.

But I didn't.

Instead I let them shuttle me from Bloomingdale's to Nordstrom to Macy's and back again, until I thought they'd wear my skin off making me try on clothes. I told Mom I didn't want to look at the sizes, but of course, once I was alone in the dressing rooms, I checked every tag.

We were back at Bloomingdale's trying on the three dresses we'd put on hold there when Grandma said she thought one of them was a little too tight in the chest and I should get the next size up so I could really show off my "girls."

Mom froze when she said this, and I could see the daggers she was shooting at Grandma, but Grandma just acted like it was no big deal.

Grandma: Well, she's got to face facts at some point. She's

a four and that's all there is to it. No sense beating around the bush. She should be proud of the beauty God gave her. I know that Jack boy won't complain.

I smiled at Mom and nodded as if to say I was fine. She took the dress out and went to get the size four. I closed the dressing room door again and stood there staring at myself in my underwear.

I was disgusting.

I was so *fat*.

A month ago I zipped into a two no problem. Now I was squeezing into a four.

I started bawling. By the time Mom got back with the dress, I was lying on the floor in the dressing room, and she had to stand me up and help me get dressed.

Grandma bought me the dress anyway. In a four.

I guess my date with Jack tomorrow night will be my last. Susan will never let him date a heifer. Just thinking about it makes me want to throw up.

Saturday, November 24
Weight: 125

Jill was perfect.

She was the perfect Clara. She was tiny and athletic and

beautiful. The guys were all as muscular as Jack and they tossed Jill up over their heads in lifts and spins that made me gasp. Misty Jenkins was a beautiful Sugar Plum Fairy, but Jill stole the show.

I sat there next to Jack feeling like a sausage stuffed in a casing. When James pulled the SUV into the driveway to pick me up, Jack met me at the door in a suit and tie. I was wearing the new dress Grandma bought me and my dress coat. It was long and black and covered up everything except my favorite black heels. He just jumped up the stairs two at a time and kissed me square on the mouth. His cheeks were flushed.

Jack: Damn. You are a sight for sore eyes.

Me: Hi.

Jack: Did you survive Thanksgiving?

Me: Barely.

Jack: Let's go watch some dudes in tights kill mice.

I laughed in spite of myself, and I felt all my worries that he wouldn't like me disappear for an instant. Rob was in the SUV and when I climbed in he made room so I could sit by Jack, who put his arm around me and nuzzled my neck.

When we got to the lobby of the theater James suggested we go and check our coats, and my stomach dropped. I tried to think of what Kim would say. This is just my disease that's worried. It's my disease trying to make me feel like I'm worthless and fat. It's my disease that's telling me I'm ugly.

Jack helped me out of my coat, but instead of turning to the girl at the coat check, he and Rob just stopped and stared. The dress Grandma had bought me had a fitted, strapless black velvet bodice with a short, flouncy skirt in red plaid taffeta. I'd worn black stockings with a seam up the back, and as I turned and caught them both staring, Rob whistled, and Jack murmured:

Merry Christmas to me . . .

I laughed and could feel a blush burning its way across both cheeks toward my ears. I felt Susan step up next to me and slide an arm across my bare shoulders.

Susan: Well, well, young lady.

Jack: I'm sorry. I know it's not polite to stare.

Susan: No, no. You should stare.

She turned to me and gave me a little squeeze.

Susan: Plumping up has made you positively *radiant*.

Jack and Rob were checking coats and James was at the bar fetching white wine. Nobody heard her say the words "plumping up" but me. The blush on my cheeks turned from one of pleasure to a sting of overwhelming shame. I don't remember exactly what happened at the ballet after intermission.

I remember knowing that Jill was beautiful and that Jack

must be stroking my leg at the hem of my skirt so I didn't feel bad about being so plump.

It's been three hours since the applause in the hall died down, and two since Jack walked me to the door and told me something very sweet I'm sure was meant to spare my feelings. Susan's words, however, are the ones still ringing in my ears:

Plumping up.

The worst part is, she's right.

Thursday, November 29
Weight: 126

Just got off the phone with Jack. When he called he sounded so distant and far away that I thought he was calling to break up with me. I got really nauseous and lay across my bed, closed my eyes, and prepared for the worst.

He said there'd been an accident. Jill was performing in the matinee this afternoon and broke her foot. It's a stress fracture. Jack says she'll be out of the show for the rest of the run.

I was so relieved he wasn't calling to break up with me because I was too plump that I immediately jumped up and pulled on some shoes.

Me: I'm coming over right this second. What can I bring her?

He was silent. My heart dropped again. Something was *wrong*.

Me: Jack?

Jack: She's not here, babe.

Me: Is she still at the hospital?

Jack: Um . . . no. Not that hospital. She just left with my parents.

Me: Where did they go?

Jack: They're taking her to a place in Arizona. It's sort of a . . . hospital. It's like . . . a rehab.

Me: A rehab?

Jack: Yeah. It's a treatment center for anorexia.

I slowly slumped back down on the bed as the weight of this settled over me. Jack was quiet, but I could hear him breathing on the phone. Then I heard him sniff. It sounded like he was crying.

Me: Jack? Are you okay? Are you there by yourself?

Jack: Yeah. I'm fine. I just . . .

His voice trailed off, and I waited, holding my breath for what would come next.

Jack: I just . . . you looked *so beautiful* last night, and I am *so glad* that you're getting *better*.

Tears sprang up in my eyes and slowly rolled down my cheeks.

Me: Do you want to come over and hang out?

Jack: Is that okay? Will your mom mind?

Me: No. Come over.

I told Mom what was going on and she was glad I'd told Jack to come over. Rob came by too for a little while but left pretty quickly. I think he felt strange watching Jack and me together. It probably made him miss Jill. He's a big clown most days, but I can tell he really cares for her and that he was really scared.

After he left, Mom called Susan and left her a voice mail, just saying that she had heard what happened and that Jack was over at our place and to let her know if she could do something or if they needed anything. Mom went to bed and left me sitting on the couch with Jack, who laid his head down on my lap and fell asleep while we were watching TV.

I sat there running my fingers through his hair with a billion thoughts zinging through my brain at the same time. After a while, he woke up and smiled at me. He stretched and sat up and gave me a kiss, then looked at his watch and said he had to get home.

Me: I could sit here and watch you sleep all night.

Jack: If we spend the night together, I'm not gonna be sleeping.

He smirked, and I messed up his hair. We walked to the

247

front door with our arms around each other. He kissed me again and asked if he could come pick me up for school in the morning. I shrugged and said sure.

Jack: See you in the morning, beautiful.

I stood at the front door in the quiet house and watched until his taillights turned the corner, then I came upstairs and started writing.

When I was sitting there on the couch with Jack it crossed my mind how lucky I was that I hadn't gotten a stress fracture from running. Jill had gotten hurt so easily. I keep thinking about what Dr. Crane said about anorexia being a disease, and I wonder if I've done permanent damage. I still haven't had my period yet. What if my body is already giving out? What if I'm putting on weight too fast? Jack says he's happy that I'm getting healthy again, but what if they keep making me gain weight? Maybe fifteen pounds is plenty.

I just can't help thinking about those big girls who sit at the back of the cafeteria at school eating bags of cheese puffs and drinking soda with sugar in it. I swear, just walking by them you could get a corn syrup contact high. Is that where I'm headed? I don't want to end up thundering around in XXL sweatshirts covered in greasy fingerprints. I'm worried because I haven't been running at all since homecoming. Not even once. No wonder I've gained fifteen pounds so fast.

I need to go to sleep. My brain is in a spin. Reading all of
that makes me feel silly for writing it, but that's what's going on
in my head. Kim said something the other day in our group that
caught my ear:

You're only as sick as your secrets.

Maybe writing all of these thoughts down isn't enough.
Maybe I need to be talking about them more to Dr. Crane and
to the other girls in group.

Jack is the sweetest, kindest guy I have ever met. I'm a lucky
girl.

I hope Jill is okay. Wherever she is. Maybe we can learn to
help each other stay healthy just like we helped each other not
eat. That idea makes me smile.

Saturday, December 1
Weight: 128

All I could think about at the ice-skating rink was how fat
my coat made me feel. I kept catching a glimpse of myself in
the glass at the end of the rink by the snack bar. Maybe it was
because it's curved, or maybe it's because I am a whale, but my
jacket made me look like that cartoon man in the commercials
who is made out of tires.

Jack seemed not to notice, or if he did, he didn't let it stop him from holding my hand the whole time. He and Rob are really good because they play in this hockey league during the winter. They can skate backward and do these "hockey stops" where they spray ice all over the place. It was all I could do to stand up at the beginning, but Jack was really patient, and by the end I was doing okay. Geoff and Vanessa came with us, and it was nice to be out with everybody, although it was weird not having Jill there. She's really good on the ice. She took lessons until we were in junior high, when she stopped to concentrate on ballet.

I've been talking a lot about my secrets at group this past week. I tell them almost everything I write down in here.

Almost.

If I just keep a few secrets that means I'm just a little bit sick, right?

I've been running again. I figure if I'm going to eat this many calories every day, I can at least run a couple of miles. I haven't told Mom I'm doing it yet. Or anybody, for that matter. I'm just running when I get home from school.

Also, I've decided I'm not drinking any calories. That seems like a fair rule. I'll eat whatever Mom gives me, but I'm just not going to drink anything with sugar in it. That's empty calories anyway.

It's funny how you can fool lots of people into thinking

you're completely better. Mom is thrilled with my progress. Dr. Nash told me my hair is coming back in really well where it had gotten thin at my temples, and she said once I was back up at 130 I'd be out of the woods.

I didn't fool Jack.

When the Zamboni came out to resurface the ice, Geoff and Vanessa went into the snack bar to get hot chocolate. Rob was talking to Jill outside. She gets to make two phone calls on Saturdays. I haven't gotten one of them yet. She calls her mom and Rob. When Jack ordered two hot chocolates, I put my hand on his arm.

Me: I want some Earl Grey tea.

He paused, and this funny look crossed his face. He turned back to the counter and changed the order. We walked over to a little table in the corner to wait for our drinks.

Jack: You're doing it again, aren't you?

I looked at him, my eyes wide and searching. Trying to appear innocent. Looking very caught.

Me: What? No. I'm . . . Jack. Look at me. I look like a blimp in this coat. I've gained so much weight since homecoming I'm practically—

Jack: I'm not a moron.

He wasn't angry, his tone was quiet, but his eyes were on fire.

Jack: I know there's a difference between the way you eat and the way you think.

I looked down at my skates. I just wanted him to hug me, to tell me how beautiful I was, that everything would be okay.

Our drinks were ready. He got up to get them, and when he came back, Geoff and Vanessa joined us. We all talked and laughed, and Rob came back in with a report on Jill. We finished skating, and Jack kept holding my hand. He didn't bring it up again, but when he dropped me off just now he kissed me and looked at me for a long time.

Jack: I just want you to be careful.

Me: I *am* being careful.

Jack: I don't want to lose you.

Me: You won't. *Look* at me. I'm *better*.

He nodded, but I could see the doubt behind his eyes.

Tuesday, December 11
Weight: 125

I stopped writing in this journal so I could stop sharing at group. Something about writing down what I'm doing makes it real. I've been restricting my calories again. I've been using the app to make sure I burn off most of what I'm eating. I've been running before Mom gets home from work and doing the cardio workout Jill showed me in my room early in the morning and again at night after Mom goes to bed.

The weight is coming off again. Just losing a few pounds last week made me feel like all my clothes fit better.

At group, Kim asked me if I was okay. We have to tell our weight every time we go, and she's been paying attention. So has Vanessa. At lunch today, she saw me throwing away most of my salad. I thought everyone had gotten over the idea that I wasn't eating enough. For a while there it was like I got a round of applause every time I swallowed a bite. Gradually, everybody stopped staring at me while I lifted a fork to my mouth. No such luck today.

Vanessa: Are you throwing all of that away?

Me: What? I'm full.

Vanessa: Of *what*? You barely touched that.

I couldn't handle it. I completely snapped.

Me: Damn it, Vanessa. Butt out! You're not my mom. You're not my doctor. This is none of your *business*.

I ran out of the cafeteria in tears.

Jack followed me. I was unlocking my car door in the parking lot when he caught up with me. As I tried to pull the door open he reached over my shoulder and pushed it closed.

I turned around and slumped against the car door and crossed my arms. It wasn't until I looked up at him that I realized there were tears running down his cheeks.

Jack: What do I have to do?

Me: This is not about you.

Jack: Yes. Yes, it *is* about me. You made it about me.

Me: How?

Jack: By being so beautiful. By being so smart and funny and such a good kisser. I fell in love with you. So this *is* about me now. I love you and I want you to know that, not up in your head, or in some greeting card sort of way. I want you to *know it* in your bones. This is my business, dammit. *You* are my business.

His cheeks were flushed, and his breath was coming out in sharp staccato bursts of white steam against the cold December air. I wanted to say I was sorry, but I couldn't.

Me: I'm not trying to hurt you.

Jack: But you *are*. When you hurt someone I love, you *hurt me*. Don't you get it? I *love you*.

I wanted to hug him. I wanted to tell him I would try harder, but I didn't. Everything he was saying was being drowned out by a voice that whispered into my ear: He doesn't really mean this. He's just being nice. He knows his mom is right. You're plump. If you really care for him, you'll walk away.

You'll spare him the humiliation of having a fat girlfriend.

He snapped me out of my thoughts when he reached up and gently touched my face.

Me: How could you love me like this?

When I said those words, I saw the same sad, faraway look that had sprung into his eyes at the ice rink when I changed my order from hot chocolate to tea.

Jack: I love you just the way you are. Doesn't that count for anything?

All I could do was shrug. He shook his head and took a step backward.

Jack: I don't understand how that doesn't make everything better. I keep thinking if I love you hard enough, or well enough, that you'll learn how to love yourself the way I do.

He turned to walk into the school building, then stopped and looked back.

Jack: I'm not giving up on you. Don't you give up on me.

Wednesday, December 19
Weight: 121

When Dad started crying, something in me snapped.

Jack called Mom. Dr. Crane called Mom. Dr. Nash called Mom. Mom called Dad.

Mom found me organizing all the clothing in my closet by color at 2 a.m. this morning. She woke up to go to the bathroom and saw the light on in my room. She took one look and knew the obsessive-compulsive part of this was back in full swing.

Today when I got home from school, she and Dad were sitting in the living room. Dad had a pamphlet and a website pulled up on his iPad. It's not the place Jill went to. That place is a gazillion dollars per day, but this place looks nice enough. It's here in town and Dr. Crane recommended it. Our insurance will cover it for twenty-two days.

At first I told them no way. I told them I was doing just fine. Then Dad asked if he could see my phone. He pulled out my laptop. He clicked to the website Jill had shown me. He'd found it in the history. I'd just posted a screen shot last night from CalorTrack. It showed that I'd done a cardio routine twice and run three miles after I got home from group. It also showed I'd only eaten 1,200 calories—most of which I'd burned off from overexercise.

I opened my mouth to defend myself. I was going to yell at him for snooping on my computer. When I looked up at him, there were tears running down his face.

I've never seen my dad cry before. Even when he was here and miserable and leaving Mom. Even when his dad died when

I was in sixth grade. Something inside me decided not to fight him.

I check into Hope House the day after Christmas next week.

Tuesday, December 25
Weight: 119

Dad came over this morning to open presents with me. He and Mom have figured out how to be nice to each other for my sake, I guess. Dad made pancakes for us and made sure I ate one. I mainly cut it up in little pieces and scooted it around in the syrup until it fell apart.

He's coming back tomorrow to help Mom take me to Hope House. Mom is visibly relieved that I'm going. She's probably glad not to have to feel like she's checking up on me every waking moment.

I woke up really early this morning and did my cardio routine twice. I know I shouldn't, but I can't help it. No matter how hard I tried, I knew I'd have to eat something really fattening today and if I didn't want to lose my mind, I had to get a jump on the calories.

I tried to get excited about Christmas presents this morning. I put on my biggest smile and squealed at the appropriate times when I opened my gifts. Dad went all out. I got a new iPad and a ton of gift certificates. Mom and Grandma went back to Bloomingdale's and got a bunch of the clothes I'd tried on there. By anyone's estimation, today was a success as far as loot goes, but the best thing I got was from Jack. He went with Susan and James to Arizona so they could spend Christmas with Jill, and then bring her back home in a couple of days. Mom usually crams my stocking full of lip balm and socks and candy. This morning, after I dumped out all of the usual stuff, I felt a heavy lump in the toe and pulled out a little blue box. It was a silver locket in the shape of a heart, and on the inside he'd engraved four words:

Just like you are.

I slipped it around my neck and for the first time I decided maybe I could face going to this treatment center. I logged on to the forum as weigh2go and there in the middle of all the posts about staying strong against Christmas candy and how not eating was the best gift you could give yourself, I wrote:

Going to get help tomorrow. I want to get better.

I clicked send, and as I did a new picture popped up at the top of the forum. It was posted under Jill's username, and it was a snapshot of the two of us at the pool back in seventh grade. We were tan and covered in freckles. My hair was frizzy, and hers was wet. We still had the round chubby cheeks of elementary school students, and we were laughing so hard our eyes were tiny slits. Neither one of us would have passed for "skinny" in this picture, but underneath it, Jill had typed a single word:

Beautiful.

Thursday, December 27
Weight: 122

Getting moved in was sad and exhausting. I'm sharing a room with a girl named Patricia who keeps to herself. We talked for a little while last night, and she said she's been here for a week. She's a bulimic and says she can't stop throwing up her meals. She's having major dental problems because the constant stomach acid in her mouth has eaten the enamel off her teeth. She's missing a tooth and the rest are a weird yellow color.

This morning we all had breakfast together. Everyone has to eat everything on their plate, no questions asked. My heart was racing as I shoveled in the eggs and oatmeal. I felt bloated by the time I stood up from the table. We all have chores assigned to us, and mine is to help wash dishes in the kitchen. I felt like a cow shuffling around the kitchen taking plates and glasses out of the dish dryer and putting them away.

After that I had my first appointment with my new therapist. It's a woman this time. She told me to call her Sharon. I like her, but I miss Dr. Crane. I talked about him and it turns out Sharon knows him. When I asked her how, she smiled.

Sharon: I'm here to help girls like you who are struggling with anorexia because I struggled with it too. Dr. Crane saved my life.

Me: You were an anorexic?

Sharon: Still am. But I've been recovered for over ten years now.

This startled me.

Me: So . . . you mean . . . I'll never get over this? I'll have to deal with it for the rest of my life?

Sharon: Anorexia is a disease. You can keep it in remission if you do the right things, but there is no cure. There's a line that you cross with any compulsive behavior. Once you cross that line, there's no going back. If you work hard, you can recover, but you'll always have to stay on your guard.

This scared me. I thought about the picture Jill had posted of us online a couple days ago. I wanted to go back. I wanted to have a rewind/erase button on the last year of my life. I wanted to never have crossed the line into this disease.

Me: How do I start?

Sharon: You start by using your *words* to tell me what's

wrong. Right now you're using your body. I'm going to ask you to use your *words* to tell me about what you're feeling instead.

This made sense to me—it was like a lightbulb clicked on in my head. Dr. Crane and I had talked a lot about what I was feeling, but he'd never put it like this. Or maybe he had, and I just hadn't heard him.

We talked for a long time during my session about what I was feeling about my dad, my mom, Jack, Jill, Vanessa. It wasn't so much about food or eating or how I looked on the outside. It was a conversation about how I felt on the inside.

When time was up, Sharon smiled and told me I was doing great.

Sharon: Remember, not eating, starving yourself, overexercise, those things aren't the problem. Those things are a *symptom* of the real problem. That's what you're here to figure out. What is the real problem? Once you know, we'll find other ways for you to deal with it that don't involve hurting yourself.

I had to come right back to my room to write that down. It sounded so exciting to hear her say it like that. When I was talking to Sharon I remembered back to a time when I wasn't all worried about the way I looked around Jack or other boys. Even just last summer at the pool I wasn't so focused on my weight. I think if I can find that place again, I'll be able to beat this. Hearing Sharon lay out a plan for finding the real problem made me feel so relieved. Like there's hope—a light at the end of the tunnel.

For the first time tonight, I feel like maybe I can win.

Tuesday, January 1
Weight: 124

I got called into Sharon's office this morning, and when I walked in, Mom was standing there. Turns out the insurance company reversed the preauthorization for my stay here at Hope House. Mom and Dad can't afford to keep me here, even though it's not as expensive as some of the other places.

Sharon and Mom and I had a session and talked about the issues I've been going over with Sharon every day in our individual sessions and sharing about on a group level. It was really hard to talk about how I blamed Mom for not staying slim enough and I blamed Dad for leaving. I could tell that it was killing Mom to take me out of this place, but on the way home, we talked about it, and I feel like I understand how my brain was tricking me into hurting myself.

Mom and I made a plan. I'm going back to the outpatient program with Dr. Crane and the group therapy meetings with Kim. I texted Kim as soon as I was in the car, and she called me and I told her what happened. Kim told me I could call her anytime and that she'd see me at group on Thursday.

When Mom and I got home, we headed straight to my room. We threw out all of my old fashion magazines. I used to keep every issue neatly stacked under my bed, and I'd look at the pictures and obsess about how I wasn't as skinny as the models. We hung sheets over the mirror in my room so I'm not tempted to obsess about how I look every time I walk past it.

Then Mom suggested we go get manicures, and on the way to our usual salon, she made a wrong turn.

Me: Where are we going?

Mom: Thought it would be fun for Jill to come with us.

I was nervous until I saw Jill. She was tan and smiling and had gained about twelve pounds while she was gone. She looked like a different person—one that I remembered from a long time ago.

She came running down the front walk, and I jumped out of the car and gave her a big hug. Jack wasn't far behind her. Soon I was squeezed in his big arms.

Me: Thank you for the locket.

Jack: Every time you think about not eating, I want you to read that.

I smiled. Jill was already in the backseat.

Jill: I'm sorry, but that's all the time we have for this episode

263

of canoodling on the driveway. Tune in next time when we're back with beautiful nail enamel.

And just like that, everything seemed like it was going to be okay. Jack blew us a kiss as Mom pulled out of the driveway.

Tuesday, January 8
Weight: 126

I can't believe how much fun school was today. It was like the old gang was back together. Jill and I have been hanging out all the time again, and last weekend, Geoff and Vanessa joined us for a movie. This time when Rob and Jack ordered concessions Jill got popcorn and I got a hot dog. We even made Jack share his Junior Mints. It's sort of like I've been remembering myself—the old me who wasn't obsessed with food.

I've been sharing about all of this in group, and Dr. Crane even asked me to tell everybody in my own words about what I'd learned with Sharon at Hope House. Kim had a big smile on her face as I talked about how my anorexia was a symptom, not the problem, and by the time I was done sharing, there were tears in her eyes—and mine.

Sharon told me before I left Hope House that it was a good

thing to journal whenever I had feelings come up—especially hard ones—but that she wanted to make sure I wasn't tracking my weight or my food too obsessively, so I think this might be my last entry for a while. I'm still going to go to group, and I'm still going to be seeing Dr. Crane, but as I think about everything this food diary was supposed to be in the beginning and what it became later, it seems like a good idea to take a break. Writing in this journal has been all about calories and weight and food and restriction.

I feel like I'm walking into a new chapter of my life now— one that isn't restricted at all. It's a place where I feel free to love myself exactly the way I am.

Wednesday, January 16
Weight: 126

So much for not keeping track anymore.

Misty Jenkins stopped by our lunch table at school today. She took one look at Jill, sitting there all tan and happy, and couldn't stop herself.

Misty: Hey, Jill! Wow! You look so . . . tan.

It sounded nice, but it wasn't. The word "tan" was delivered instead of the word "heavy," which is what Misty was thinking.

Jack: Hey, twinkle toes. Get lost.

Rob: Yeah, don't you have some fairies to wrangle or sugarplums to eat or something?

Misty's smile was sickly sweet.

Misty: You guys are so funny. No fairies this spring. Just swans. Didn't Jill tell you we're doing *Swan Lake*?

Vanessa didn't get what was happening and took the bait.

Vanessa: No! Really? Oh, that's so exciting! I love that ballet.

Misty: Glad your ankle is better, Jill. Too bad about everything else. You're way too heavy to be a lead now.

Jack jumped up so fast his chair skidded into the wall of the cafeteria.

Jack: Get out of here. Now.

Misty smirked and glanced down at me.

Misty: Sure thing, Jack. If you ever get tired of being seen with that little scarecrow girl, give me a call.

I thought I would throw up. I left everything on the table, grabbed my purse, and ran into the bathroom. I locked a stall door and sat there crying.

When I got home tonight, I took the sheet off the mirror, got undressed, and really looked at myself in the mirror for the first time in several weeks. What I saw horrified me.

Misty is right: I *am* a scarecrow girl. My hair is like straw, and my body looks stuffed and ragged. I have lumpy curves in all the wrong places. Why has everyone been lying to me? Maybe Misty is mean, but at least she's telling the truth.

Wednesday, January 23
Weight: 122

It's been two weeks since I started using the CalorTrack app again. I've been keeping net calories at 1,200 per day so I don't get too skinny too fast. That also allows me to eat about 1,700 calories per day, most of which I pack into lunch so that Vanessa and Jack don't get on my case about not eating. I've started doing hard runs again in the afternoon instead of going to group. This helps me burn off as much as I can, and then I do my cardio routine at night after Mom's gone to bed.

I'm glad Misty was honest with me about how I looked. I will not lose Jack. As sweet as he is, he doesn't understand what he's asking. He doesn't want a girl who weighs 135 pounds. He won't know that until he sees me, so I'm not going to let myself take that risk.

It just feels good to be back in control. I'm sort of proud of myself for recognizing all this feel-good crap for what it is: people who don't have the willpower to stay thin and beautiful.

Wednesday, February 6
Weight: 118

Mom has flipped. Dr. Crane keeps calling to tell her when I don't show up at my sessions. I told her I don't care. This is who I am. I'm a thin, beautiful girl. Jack and Vanessa ganged up on me. They pulled me aside after school the other day and told me they can tell that I'm restricting again. I told Vanessa to get lost. I held the locket around my neck up in Jack's face.

Me: So did you mean this or not?

Jack: What? Why are you being like this?

Me: Did you *mean* it? Did you actually mean that you love me *just like I am*?

Jack: Of course.

Me: *This* is me, Jack. *This* is who I am.

We have a date next week for Valentine's Day. We're supposed to double with Jill and Rob. I was just trying on clothes and saw that I have these tiny dark hairs all over my torso and arms. It's like the hair I shave off my legs, but softer. I've seen girls post about this on the forum before. I called Jill.

Me: Mayday.

Jill: Yeah?

Me: I am getting hairy like an ape.

She chuckled.

Jill: You too, huh?

Me: You mean . . . ?

Jill: Of course. Come over. I've got some wax. We'll take care of it. Can't be hirsute for Valentine's Day.

Mom wasn't home from work yet, so I drove over to her place. We waxed. It was painful, but I'm smooth as a baby's bottom now. Jill has been restricting again, too. I sensed she was, but we'd both been careful not to talk about it.

It feels like we're sitting on a powder keg—that at any minute, everyone around us might blow up. Sometimes I think it's the level of discipline that makes people so angry and upset at us for not wanting to be fat slobs. Why shouldn't we look like models? Why do you think you buy the products these girls advertise? It's not because they're better than any other product. It's because you want to *look like the girl who is selling it.*

That's why I buy stuff.

Girls who look a certain way use a certain thing. If I use that thing, I'll be as pretty as the girl who is using it in the commercial or the magazine.

This isn't rocket science. If you want to look like a girl in a magazine, you eat and exercise like one.

Why is that such a problem for my mom? For Jill's dad? For Vanessa? For Kim? For Dr. Crane? For Sharon?

Because they know they could *never* do what we're doing.

They could *never* be this disciplined. Look at Sharon. She tried to once upon a time and failed.

Miserably.

Jill and I will not fail.

Thursday, February 14
Weight: 116

Trying to get back down to my homecoming weight, but dealing with it better this time. It feels right to be wearing my skinny jeans again. Mom has gone back to working the night shift because the pay is better and she needs to up our health insurance plan so she can send me to a better treatment center.

As if I'd go.

Dad stays away now for the most part. I think it's too hard for him to see me all grown up. I am my own woman now whether he likes it or not.

I made Jack bring me home tonight after our Valentine's double date. Jill and I looked amazing, but I could tell something was different with Jack. After dinner he and Rob took us for a carriage ride around the city. We were bundled under blankets in the back, and I felt his hand on my thigh. He flinched when he touched me. I can feel a difference in the way he puts his hands on me—almost as if he is afraid I will break.

But this is who I am.

This is the best version of me.

I can tell he doesn't love me.

After the carriage ride, we were supposed to go to the top of a big hotel downtown with a rotating restaurant for dessert. I laughed when I heard this.

Me: Dessert?

Jack: Yeah . . . do you . . . not want to go?

Me: I'm not going to have any.

Jack just stopped and stared. He reached out a hand and gently touched the silver heart hanging around my neck.

Jack: Okay. I guess I'll take you back.

He drove me home without a word. I sat there feeling stupid. He hates my body. He should hate my body. I hate it. I wanted it to be perfect. I should have done more. I shouldn't have let them shame me into eating so much. I should've measured the food I did eat perfectly. I should have tracked the calories perfectly.

If I could just get back down to where I was that night I walked down the stairs last fall in the red dress, everything would be better. It would fix his hesitance. If I still looked like that I'd feel his desire when he touched me instead of his repulsion.

He walked me to the front door and kissed me lightly on the lips.

271

Jack: I wish you could see how beautiful you are.

When I went inside the house, I came upstairs to my room and cried tears of anger for not being good enough for him. I wanted so badly to be the perfect valentine. Instead, he could barely touch me. He was repulsed.

I'll fix this. I'll make it all better. I'm going to be a hundred pounds by spring break. He'll see then. He won't be able to take his eyes off me. I'll be perfect.

Wednesday, February 20
Weight: 115

Mom found out today that the new insurance won't cover any treatment for my anorexia. It's a "preexisting" condition. She's still vowing to send me off to a treatment camp somewhere, but I won't go. I'm looking better than I have in a long time.

I don't need a "Do This Instead" box anymore. Now that Jill's working hard to get back in shape too, we stay in touch. Anytime I'm tempted, I just text her, and vice versa. We're limiting ourselves to 500 net calories per day. That means I can eat 1,200 and burn 700 or so. My thighs don't touch anymore. I'm getting down to homecoming weight! The lower I see the number drop on the scale, the better I feel about myself.

Jill and I are doing our workout routine twice each day until spring break. It's easier on our joints and bones than running. I don't want to get a stress fracture like she did. Casting for *Swan Lake* happens the first day of spring break next month.

I don't think I have time to keep this journal anymore. There's too much other stuff to do and all writing about this does is make me focus on the wrong thoughts and feelings. I don't want to think about how I feel. I just want to do the things I know will make me feel good about myself. I've got five pounds left, and four weeks to get there. I'm on track to look perfect in my swimsuit in Jack's hot tub the first day of spring break.

I'm not going to write again until I make my goal.

Friday, March 22
Weight: 110.5

Jack is coming over tonight. He said he's got a surprise for me, but I've got a surprise for him! I'm *finally* back down to the weight I was on homecoming night. When I got home from school today Mom was on her way out the door to work. She looked at me like she was seeing a ghost and just started crying.

Mom: What is it going to take?

Me: Mom. Please. Save it.

Mom: I am trying to *save you.* I don't know what to do anymore.

She went on and on about admitting me to the hospital and how Dr. Nash said my not eating enough could be doing real damage to my heart and organs.

Mom: I just want to get you some help for your disease.

Me: Mom! I am not diseased! Can't you see? I look better than all those other Fatty McFattersons. I am thin and gorgeous.

I swear it makes me so angry. If this is a disease, more people should catch it. All they can talk about on the news is how so many Americans are obese and overweight. You'd think my mom would be *happy* that I'm not some two-ton fatso thundering around the house. But no. She can't be *happy* for me. No, no. It must be a *disease*.

I stomped up to my room and started doing my exercise routine. I got really light-headed in the middle of it and couldn't stop coughing just now. I actually coughed up some blood. It was sort of amazing. I think I'm so thin my body is digesting itself.

I logged on to the forum and posted as weigh2go:

Finally back at my goal weight. Happier than I've been in MONTHS!

Jill called me right away.

Jill: Hey! Just saw your post.

Me: I *know*, right? It's amazing.

Jill: Congrats, lady. I think we should go for a jog to celebrate.

Me: Yes! I'm going to jog over to your place.

Jill: Excellent. See you in ten?

Me: Give me fifteen. I need to change clothes.

Hopefully, there won't be any more blood. I wonder if Jill has ever coughed up blood? I'll have to ask her about it.

Friday, March 22
EMERGENCY TRANSCRIPT

Dispatch: 911. What's your emergency?

Caller: My girlfriend collapsed. I need an ambulance.

Dispatch: Where are you?

Caller: I'm on Caballeros near the corner of Alejo.

Dispatch: Sending paramedics now. What is your name?

Caller: I'm Jack.

Dispatch: Jack, when did your girlfriend collapse?

Caller: I don't know. I didn't see it happen. She was jogging over to my house, and then she didn't show up and she didn't answer her phone, so we got in the car to go to her place to check on her.

Dispatch: Is someone there with you?

Caller: Yes. My sister.

Dispatch: Is your girlfriend breathing?

Caller: I can't tell.

Dispatch: Does it look like she's sustained other injuries?

Caller: She's got blood coming out of her mouth.

Dispatch: Is she lying on her back?

Caller: Yes.

Dispatch: Can you see if her chest is rising and falling?

Caller: Not really. I think it is. Just a little.

Dispatch: Are her eyes opened or closed?

Caller: Closed.

Dispatch: And she appears to be breathing.

Caller: Yeah, but it's sorta shallow. Oh, man! Please! Hurry up!

Dispatch: Jack? The ambulance is on its way. Stay on the phone with me. Jack? Are you there?

Caller: Yes! Yes, I'm here. My sister doesn't think she's breathing anymore.

Dispatch: Jack, do you know CPR?

Caller: Yes. My sister is starting compressions.

Dispatch: Make sure that you clean her mouth out with your finger to remove any blood or debris.

Caller: Okay. Okay. I did. I'm gonna set the phone down.

Dispatch: I'll hold the line.

Caller: Okay, I blew into her mouth and my sister is doing compressions. Oh—I hear the ambulance. Here they come. And a police car just pulled up.

Dispatch: I'll let you go. Thanks, Jack.

REPORT

Case #: 13-1612

Date: Friday, March 22, ███

Deceased: ██████████

Age: 16

Sex: Female

Race: Caucasian

Summary: ██████████ was pronounced dead on the 22nd day of March ███ at 5:29 p.m. by Regina Nash, MD, at ███████ Medical Center.

Hospital #: ED#098839520

Admitted: 22nd day of March ███ at 5:04 p.m. by ambulance from street corner of Caballeros and Alejo. Admitted by R. Nash, MD.

Symptoms: Cardiac arrest, bleeding from mouth

Remarks: History of anorexia nervosa/depression

Body identified by: ██████████, decedent's mother, who was on staff in the ER at the time of arrival.

Immediate cause of death: Cardiac arrest

Due to: Anorexia nervosa

Other conditions contributing but not relating to the immediate cause of death: Natural cause

CASE REPORT

Informant: Pam Tomlin, RN

Incident:

The decedent is a 16-year-old female with a reported history of anorexia nervosa.

The decedent was last known to be alive this afternoon when her mother (an RN on duty in the emergency room when decedent arrived) left for work. Decedent spoke with a friend, Jill ████████ then hung up the phone at 4:10 p.m., then left for a 15-minute jog to friend's house. After no word from decedent at 4:30 p.m., decedent's friend and brother (decedent's boyfriend) attempted to reach decedent via phone call and text message. After receiving no replies, decedent's friend and boyfriend drove toward decedent's house to look for her. Decedent was found unconscious on the southwest corner of Caballeros and Alejo.

Paramedics were summoned by decedent's boyfriend, Jack ████████, responded, and continued CPR initiated by friend and boyfriend while transporting the decedent to the hospital. The decedent was admitted to the emergency room of ████████ Medical Center, where lifesaving efforts proved to be of no avail. Death was pronounced at 5:29 p.m., 3-22-██, by Dr. Nash.

This investigator viewed the decedent at ████████ Medical Center. Close examination revealed no indications of trauma or foul play. Clothing (light blue jogging suit) and jewelry (silver heart-shaped locket) released to ████████, decedent's mother. No additional information known by this investigator at this time.

**Turn the page for a sneak peek at
another anonymous diary.**

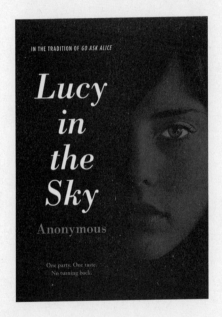

July 4

~~Dear Diary,~~

That's ridiculous. Who writes "Dear Diary" in a diary? I mean, who writes in a diary at all? Shouldn't I be blogging?

This is lame.

July 5

Okay, so this isn't going to be a diary. It's a journal. I guess that's the same thing, but "journal" sounds less like I'm riding a tricycle or something.

Yesterday was my birthday. I turned 16.

It's so weird sharing a birthday with your country. Always fireworks: never for you. Mom always plans an actual birthday dinner—usually the Saturday night after July 4th so that I can have a day where we celebrate just for me. It's fun, kinda like having two birthdays in the same week.

We're not big July 4th celebrators . . . celebrators? Celebrants? People. Whatever—we're not big on July 4th. Usually in the afternoon we have friends from school over and walk down to the beach to play volleyball. There are lots of nets at the beach just down the hill, then we haul ourselves back up the canyon to our house for a cookout in the evening. My brother, Cam, invites his friends from the varsity soccer team. Mom gets my favorite cake (the one with the berries in it).

After we gorge on grilled meat and birthday cake, we all crowd onto the balcony outside my parents' bedroom and watch the fireworks down the coast. You can see the display at the pier really well, and the ones in the cities just up the coast shoot off too. Last year Cam (nobody calls him Cameron except Mom) climbed onto the roof from the front porch so he could get a better view, but Mom freaked and said, CAMERON! Get. Down. This. Instant. Mom's big on safety.

I got a lot of cool presents yesterday. Mom got me the swimsuit I tried on at the mall last week. It's a really cute two-piece with boy shorts, and this fun, twisty top. Dad's present to me was that he's taking me to get my license this week. I've been practicing with him in the parking lot near his office at the college. He gave me a coupon for one "Full Day with Dad." On the back it says, "Good for one driving test at the DMV, followed by a celebratory meal at the restaurant of holder's choosing, and a $100 shopping spree/gift card to store of choice."

He made it himself out of red construction paper and drew this funny little stick figure on the front. It's supposed to be him. He draws curly hair on the sides of the round head so the little man is bald on top like he is. The coupon is sort of cheesy, but so is my dad. I think it's funny. And cute.

Cam got me this journal. We've been going to this yoga

class together, and the teacher is this woman named Marty with bright eyes who talks about her birds a lot. She told us to get a journal and spend a few minutes each day writing down our thoughts and feelings.

I just looked back at everything I've written, and it's mainly thoughts. Not very many feelings. I'm not sure how I feel right now. I mean, I guess I feel fine? Happy?

No, just fine. I feel fine.

I also feel like people who have birds are sort of weird.

July 6

It's funny that Cam bought me this journal. It's one of those things I would never have bought for myself but secretly wanted. I don't know how he knows that stuff. I guess that's what older brothers are supposed to do: read your mind. I mean, who actually goes out and tries the stuff that their yoga teacher says to do outside of class?

Cam got way into yoga last summer when he had a crush on this exchange student from England named Briony—like Brian with a y. (Really? Who names their kid that?) Anyway, she wouldn't give Cam the time of day, so when he found out that she went to this yoga class, he started going to the same one. He bought a mat and this little bag to carry it in and just happened to show up in her class like, Oh my God! Wow!

What a coincidence. Briony never went out with him. I didn't even know she'd gone back to London until I was teasing him about how he should be glad Briony didn't do something like synchronized swimming. He was like, Briony moved back to London right after school got out.

I asked him why he was still going to yoga, and he said he really liked it. And he said I should come.

I'm not sure why I did, really. I guess I was just bored last summer. But now we go to yoga together. It's this really great studio a block off the Promenade, and they run it on donations. You just pay what you can or what you think the class is worth. I didn't think I'd like it at first. It was hard, and I got sweaty and slipped on my mat and couldn't do any of the poses. But I sorta like spending time with Cam.

Who am I writing that to? It's not like anyone is reading this but me. This is exactly how it feels when Grams asks me to pray over dinner. I feel like I'm saying all this stuff that is bouncing back at me off the ceiling and landing in the spinach salad.

Cam probably didn't have to read my mind about wanting a journal at all. He's really smart. His early acceptance letter to this great college up north came last week. He's going to be a biochem major, which just makes me want to lie down on the floor and curl up in a ball. He's a brainiac. And on top of it he's nice and enthusiastic—which has a tendency to be dangerous.

Last semester Mom was always telling me to ask Cam for help with my geometry homework. I did, but instead of telling me what to do, Cam always talks and talks and talks. It's like he knows so much about stuff and likes math so much that he has to say it all instead of just the answer.

I stopped asking questions. It sort of annoyed me. Just did it myself, and didn't really understand it. I got a C in geometry. You'd have thought I'd flown a plane into a building. (That's bad to say, I guess. I mean, I know people died and everything, but it was a really long time ago.)

Dad came unglued. He's the chairman of the music department at the college where he works. He made me sign up for tutoring this summer with a student that his friend in the math department recommended. Our session starts in a few minutes. I was relieved when Nathan showed up the first time. I was afraid I'd get stuck with some weird math girl.

Nathan is a freshman. He's from Nebraska and has brown hair that's cut short. He works out a lot, and he wears these polo shirts with sleeves that are tight right around his biceps. I just stare at his arms a lot instead of listening when he's trying to help me find the answer.

I wish somebody would just tell me the answer.

Nathan's here. Gotta go.

Later . . .

OMG.

I TOTALLY JUST INVITED NATHAN TO MY BIRTHDAY DINNER.

OMG OMG OMG OMG

And

He

Said

YES!

This is totally crazy. I can't believe I actually said the words out loud. I didn't mean to. We were just sitting at the dining room table and he was talking about the hypotenuse of a right angle, and while he was looking at the protractor he was using to draw lines, I was staring at the lines of his jaw and noticed that they were almost a right angle, and the hypotenuse of the right angle of his jaw was this line in his cheek with a dimple in the middle that he gets when he smiles, and then I heard myself saying, You should come to my birthday dinner on Saturday, and then I realized that Mom was looking RIGHT AT ME like my hair was on fire, and I realized that I'd just invited an 18-year-old over for dinner in FRONT OF MY MOTHER. OMG. I just wanted to CRAWL UNDER THE TABLE.

But he stopped with his pencil stuck into the protractor and looked up, and then glanced over at Mom like he was looking to see if she'd heard, and she smiled at him, sort of weakly. I guess he took that to mean that it was okay with her 'cause he looked me right in the eye and said, Sure. That'd be fun. Now look at this triangle.

I tried to look at the triangle for the rest of the half hour, but I have no idea what he was saying. When he left, I walked him to the door, and Mom said, Nathan, come by around 7:30. He said, Sure thing, and you can call me Nate. He waved at me before he got in his pickup truck and said, See you this weekend. Then, he drove away. Just like that.

I went running back up to my bedroom and buried my head in my pillow and did one of those silent screams where you just breathe out really hard, but with no sound; it's sort of a soft roar, but the excitement on the inside of me made it feel like my head would explode.

I could hear my heart pounding in my ears, and I took a couple of deep breaths and then I remembered what Marty said in yoga this morning about trying to meditate and how to focus on the breath, so I sat down on the floor and crossed my legs like Marty does in front of class, and I closed my eyes and took really deep breaths and tried not to think about Nate. I could do it for about 5 breaths at a time, but then I'd see that line with the dimple in it behind my eyelids, and then the rest of his right-angle jaw would appear and I'd see a triangle fill in the space on his face.

I mean, it's really no big deal. My dad is two years older than my mom. Nate's only 18, and I'm 16, and it's not like he would be robbing the cradle or anything.

I think I really like him.

OMG I CAN'T BELIEVE THAT NATE IS COMING TO DINNER ON SATURDAY.

July 8

I was just standing in my mirror trying on a couple of different options for tonight. I passed my driver's test and got my license yesterday (YAY! OMG. Finally!), then Dad and I went shopping on the Promenade. I'm a really good bargain shopper. I worked at the Gap part-time last summer and I learned to never EVER pay full-price for anything 'cause they just mark it down every two weeks. Primary, secondary, clearance. Primary, secondary, clearance. Every week on Tuesday night the markdowns would come through from the home office, and we'd all run around with those price-tag guns the next morning, marking down tops that some poor dope had paid $20 more for 12 hours ago. So, anyway, I got a lot of great stuff. Even Dad was surprised with how many items I got for $100. Well, then

I splurged a little and added $40 from my savings to get these supercute sandals that I'd been wanting.

Anyway, I have all this stuff to try on, and I felt myself doing that thing I do where I put on, like, 12 different outfits and stand there and pick every single one of them apart, and I end up standing in front of the mirror in my underwear with this pile of really cute clothes with the tags still on them lying on the floor. I had just put on the second skirt I bought and could tell I was about to find something wrong with it, and then I just stopped, looked at myself, and thought: Don't be that girl.

I just don't want to be that chick who is always staring at herself in the mirror whining about how she looks and having a meltdown in the fitting room. I mean, I'm not a model or anything, but I think I look okay. I have already showered and straightened my hair. It's not frizzy or even curly really—just has some waves, and when you live this close to the waves it can get wavy. (God. Stupid joke.) Whatever, I stepped away from the mirror and saw my journal sitting on my desk, and I thought I'd write about it. I mean, this is a feeling. I'm not sure what kinds of feelings I'm supposed to be writing about in here, but maybe this is what crazy Marty the bird lady was talking about.

I'm SO EXCITED about Nate coming over and I want to

look really hot, but the excitement also feels like nervousness, like I'm going to barf or something. Mom is downstairs putting a marinade on some shrimp that she's going to have Dad grill, and the smell when I walked through the kitchen made me feel like I was going to hurl up my toenails—and I LOVE shrimp.

I know I look good in this skirt. Dad told me it looked "far out" when I came out of the dressing room to check it out in the mirror. He said this in his I'm-being-a-little-too-loud-so-the-other-people-present-will-hear-me-and-think-I'm-hilarious-when-really-I'm-just-torturing-my-daughter voice. I told him to please be quiet and offer his opinions only regarding possible escape routes in the case of a fire, or a random stampede of wild bison. In all other matters, I respectfully asked him to please refrain from speaking to me until we had reached the cash wrap.

I looked in the mirror again just now. This skirt totally works.

Weird how excited and scared feel like the same thing.

July 8—11:30 p.m.
I shoulda known.

I shoulda known when he walked up the front steps with flowers and handed them to Mom.

But he brought me a card with a joke about having pi on

my birthday instead of cake (guh-rooooan) and it had a $25 gift card for iTunes in it. Which was cool and so sweet of him, but he just signed his name. Shoulda known when he didn't write anything personal. Just "Happy B-Day! Nate."

But he was really funny and sweet at dinner. He sat across from me and told us all this hilarious story about when he was growing up in Nebraska and he and his brother raised sheep for the county fair. (Yes. Apparently people still raise animals and take them to fairs where they win ribbons and titles and scholarships. Thank you, CHARLOTTE'S WEB.)

One morning he and his brother went out to scoop food out of these big 25-pound sacks of feed for the sheep, and there was a mouse in one of the bags that ran up his little brother's jacket sleeve. He was telling us about how he thought his brother had been possessed by a demon because he kept screaming and shaking his arms and beating at his chest and running around in a circle while the mouse wriggled around inside his shirt. We were all crying, we were laughing so hard, and Cam almost inhaled a bite of shrimp, which sent him on a coughing fit that made the rest of us laugh even harder.

He jumped up and helped me clear the table when Mom asked who wanted dessert. When Mom told him he didn't need to do that, he smiled at me and said, Oh yes, ma'am, I do. My mama'd fly in from Grand Island and smack me if I didn't.

When we were in the kitchen, I started rinsing plates and he loaded them into the dishwasher like he lived here. We were laughing and joking around and no one mentioned geometry. He was so easy to talk to, easy to be near. I didn't feel nervous even once. I couldn't help but wonder what it would feel like if we were married and this was our house and we were loading the dishwasher together. That's probably stupid, but it made me feel hopeful inside, like maybe something like that was possible.

When Nate bent over to put the final plate in the dishwasher, a necklace fell out of his shirt. It had a tiny key on it, and I was about to ask him where he got it, but Mom came into the kitchen to get some coffee mugs and the French press. Nate tucked the necklace back into his polo before I could ask him about it, but I shoulda known.

There's a long porch on the back of our house that looks over the bottom of the canyon out to the water. We ate dessert out there. Dad lit the candles in the big lanterns on the table outside. Cam sat next to Nate and they talked soccer. The flicker made their skin glow like they were on the beach at sunset. Nate looked all sun-kissed and happy. I felt a foot nudge mine just for a second under the table and my heart started racing. I was glad that it was just the candles outside in the dark 'cause I started to blush like crazy. I thought maybe Nate had touched my foot, and I kept sliding mine a little bit closer toward him under the table, but his foot never touched mine again.

It was almost 10 when he pulled out his phone and checked it, then said, Whoa. I gotta go.

I felt really bummed all of a sudden, and then silly. What was I hoping? That he'd stay and walk me down to the beach? He stood up and shook my dad's hand, then gave Cam one of those weird hugs that guys give each other where they grab hands like they're gonna shake and then lean in and hug with their arms caught in between them. He kissed my mom on the cheek and told her what a good cook she was.

Then he looked right at me and said, Will you walk me to my truck?

I got so many butterflies in my stomach, I thought they might start flying out of my ears. I said SURE, and realized that nobody had really heard him ask that because Mom was pouring more wine and Dad was pouring more coffee and Cam was texting somebody. So I slipped into the house and out the front door.

He'd parked on the street, and when he got to the door of his pickup, he leaned against it and looked up at the sky and said, Huh.

I said, What?

He told me that in Nebraska at this time of night you

could see lots of stars. I followed his gaze up to the sky, but I knew there wouldn't be any stars. Out here, the sky just glows this weird purply color even on the darkest night here. It's the light pollution bouncing off of the marine layer, I said. It's what happens at night when 8 million people get jammed up against the ocean. I turned around and stood next to him with my back up against the truck.

He said it was funny how you always hear about all the stars in Los Angeles, but at night in Nebraska, it's like the sky is covered with diamonds. Then he looked over at me, and I don't know what happened, but I just knew that I had to feel his lips on mine. So I leaned in and kissed him.

Nate jumped like I'd shot him with a taser. He said, WHOA, what are you doing? OMG! I was SO EMBARRASSED I couldn't even LOOK at him. It was like we were having this PERFECT night, and then BLAM-O: I broke the spell. I was blushing and stammering and then I felt the tears come to my eyes, and I didn't wait. I just sprinted back across the street toward the house. I was not going to let him see me cry.

As my foot hit the curb on the other side of the street, he said WAIT!

There was something in the way he said it that made me turn around. And then he shook his head and smacked his forehead, and he walked over to me, and just looked at me.

He pushed my hair over my shoulder and said, No. I'm sorry.

He told me that I had come along two years too late. And that I was beautiful. And that he has a girlfriend.

I shoulda thought about that. I shoulda never invited him to dinner tonight.

I shoulda known.